MACMILLAN SHORT STORIES

Family Matters

Bill Lucas and Brian Keaney

MACMILLAN

First published 1990

Published by
MACMILLAN EDUCATION LTD
Houndmills, Basingstoke, Hampshire RG21 2XS
and London
Companies and representatives
throughout the world

Printed in Hong Kong

British Library Cataloguing in Publication Data
Family matters. – (Macmillan short story
anthology; no. 2)
1. Short stories in English, 1945 –
Anthologies – for schools
I. Lucas, Bill   II. Keaney, Brian
823'.01'08 [FS]
ISBN 0-333-48360-X

Contents

Preface

This is a new kind of short-story collection. Instead of the larger number of stories normally included in anthologies, only six have been selected. Instead of 'notes' or 'follow-up material' added on at the end of the book, a variety of spoken and written tasks have been devised to help develop an understanding of each story as it is read. Thus the book falls naturally into six sections, each of which contains:

● a story – each one representing a different cultural perspective;

● non-literary and factual material – for example, newspaper articles and interviews, maps – to help students gain a fuller understanding of the cultural or geographical background;

● photographs;

● literary extracts, to deepen understanding of themes, characters, ideas and styles and to encourage their further exploration.

Throughout the book there is a variety of tasks of different lengths and complexity. These are always integral to the stories and their follow-up work. Suggestions have been made as to the skill areas which might be developed in each task. However, it is anticipated that they will frequently be amended by teachers or used to practise different skill areas.

A number of written assignments follow each story. They are intended to encourage the range of responses appropriate for GCSE English or English Literature coursework. It is assumed that students and their teachers will be involved in the drafting of assignments even though lack of space in this book prevents detailed assistance on this being included.

The assignments at the end of the book are particularly suitable for more extended study of the stories in the selection. As with the rest of the material, they are also suitable for independent study outside the classroom.

Secrets

Bernard MacLaverty

He had been called to be there at the end. His Great Aunt Mary had been dying for some days now and the house was full of relatives. He had just left his girlfriend home – they had been studying for 'A' levels together – and had come back to the house to find all the lights spilling onto the lawn and a sense of purpose which had been absent from the last few days.

He knelt at the bedroom door to join in the prayers. His knees were on the wooden threshold and he edged them forward onto the carpet. They had tried to wrap her fingers around a crucifix but they kept loosening. She lay low on the pillow and her face seemed to have shrunk by half since he had gone out earlier in the night. Her white hair was damped and pushed back from her forehead. She twisted her head from side to side, her eyes closed. The prayers chorused on, trying to cover the sound she was making deep in her throat. Someone said about her teeth and his mother leaned over her and said, 'That's the pet', and took her dentures from her mouth. The lower half of her face seemed to collapse. She half opened her eyes but could not raise her eyelids enough and showed only crescents of white.

'Hail Mary full of grace . . .' the prayers went on. He closed his hands over his face so that he would not have to look but smelt the trace of his girlfriend's handcream from his hands. The noise, deep and guttural, that his aunt was making became intolerable to him. It was as if she were drowning. She had lost all the dignity he knew her to have. He got up from the floor and stepped between the others who were kneeling and went into her sitting-room off the same landing.

He was trembling with anger or sorrow, he didn't know which. He sat in the brightness of her big sitting-room at the oval table and waited for something to happen. On the table was a cut-glass vase of irises, dying because she had been in bed for over a week. He sat staring at them. They were withering from the tips inward, scrolling themselves delicately, brown and neat. Clearing up after themselves. He stared at them for a long time until he heard the sounds of women weeping from the next room.

His aunt had been small – her head on a level with his when she sat at her table – and she seemed to get smaller each year. Her skin fresh, her hair white and waved and always well washed. She wore no jewellery except a cameo ring on the third finger of her right hand and, around her neck, a gold locket on a chain. The white classical profile on the ring was almost worn through and had become translucent and indistinct. The boy had noticed the ring when she had read to him as a child. In the beginning fairy tales, then as he got older extracts from famous novels, *Lorna Doone*, *Persuasion*, *Wuthering Heights* and her favourite extract, because she read it so often, Pip's meeting with Miss Havisham from *Great Expectations*. She would sit with him on her knee, her arms around him and holding the page flat with her hand. When he was bored he would interrupt her and ask about the ring. He loved hearing her tell of how her grandmother had given it to her as a brooch and she had had a ring made from it. He would try to count back to see how old it was. Had her grandmother got it from *her* grandmother? And if so what had she turned it into? She would nod her head from side to side and say, 'How would I know a thing like that?' keeping her place in the closed book with her finger.

'Don't be so inquisitive,' she'd say. 'Let's see what happens next in the story.'

One day she was sitting copying figures into a long narrow book with a dip pen when he came into her room. She didn't look up but when he asked her a question she just said, 'Mm?' and went on writing. The vase of irises on the oval table vibrated slightly as she wrote.

'What is it?' She wiped the nib on blotting paper and looked up at him over her reading glasses.

'I've starting collecting stamps and Mamma says you might have some.'

'Does she now—?'

She got up from the table and went to the tall walnut bureau-bookcase standing in the alcove. From a shelf of the bookcase she took a small wallet of keys and selected one for the lock. There was a harsh metal shearing sound as she pulled the desk flap down. The writing area was covered with green leather which had dog-eared at the corners. The inner part was divided into pigeon holes, all bulging with papers. Some of them, envelopes, were gathered in batches nipped at the waist with elastic bands. There were postcards and bills and cash-books. She pointed to the postcards.

'You may have the stamps on those,' she said. 'But don't tear them. Steam them off.'

She went back to the oval table and continued writing. He sat on the arm of the chair looking through the picture postcards – torchlight processions at Lourdes, brown photographs of town centres, dull black and whites of beaches backed by faded hotels.

Then he turned them over and began to sort the stamps. Spanish, with a bald man, French with a rooster, German with funny jerky print, some Italian with what looked like a chimney-sweep's bundle and a hatchet.

'These are great,' he said. 'I haven't got any of them.'

'Just be careful how you take them off.'

'Can I take them downstairs?'

'Is your mother there?'

'Yes.'

'Then perhaps it's best if you bring the kettle up here.'

He went down to the kitchen. His mother was in the morning room polishing silver. He took the kettle and the flex upstairs. Except for the dipping and scratching of his Aunt's pen the room was silent. It was at the back of the house overlooking the orchard and the sound of the traffic from the main road was distant and muted. A tiny rattle began as the kettle warmed up, then it bubbled and steam gushed quietly from its spout. The cards began to curl slightly in the jet of steam but she didn't seem to be watching. The stamps peeled moistly off and he put them in a saucer of water to flatten them.

'Who is Brother Benignus?' he asked. She seemed not to hear. He asked again and she looked over her glasses.

'He was a friend.'

His flourishing signature appeared again and again. Sometimes Bro Benignus, sometimes Benignus and once Iggy.

'Is he alive?'

'No, he's dead now. Watch the kettle doesn't run dry.'

When he had all the stamps off he put the postcards together and replaced them in the pigeon-hole. He reached over towards the letters but before his hand touched them his aunt's voice, harsh for once, warned.

'A-A-A,' she moved her pen from side to side. 'Do-not-touch,' she said and smiled. 'Anything else, yes! That section, no!' She resumed her writing.

The boy went through some other papers and found some photographs. One was of a beautiful girl. It was very old-fashioned but he could see that she was beautiful. The picture was a pale brown oval set on a white square of card. The edges of the oval were misty. The girl in the photograph was young and had dark, dark hair scraped severely back and tied like a knotted rope on the top of her head – high arched eyebrows, her nose straight and thin, her mouth slightly smiling, yet not smiling – the way a mouth is after smiling. Her eyes looked out at him dark and knowing and beautiful.

'Who is that?' he asked.

'Why? What do you think of her?'

'She's all right.'

'Do you think she is beautiful?' The boy nodded.

'That's me,' she said. The boy was glad he had pleased her in return for the stamps.

Other photographs were there, not posed ones like Aunt Mary's but Brownie snaps of laughing groups of girls in bucket hats like German helmets and coats to their ankles. They seemed tiny faces covered in clothes. There was a photograph of a young man smoking a cigarette, his hair combed one way by the wind against a background of sea.

'Who is that in the uniform?' the boy asked.

'He's a soldier,' she answered without looking up.

'Oh,' said the boy. 'But who is he?'

'He was a friend of mine before you were born,' she said. Then added, 'Do I smell something cooking? Take your stamps and off you go. That's the boy.'

The boy looked at the back of the picture of the man and saw in black spidery ink 'John, Aug '15 Ballintoye'.

'I thought maybe it was Brother Benignus,' he said. She looked at him not answering.

'Was your friend killed in the war?'

At first she said no, but then changed her mind.

'Perhaps he was,' she said, then smiled. 'You are far too inquisitive. Put it to use and go and see what is for tea. Your mother will need the kettle.' She came over to the bureau and helped tidy the photographs away. Then she locked it and put the keys on the shelf.

'Will you bring me up my tray?'

The boy nodded and left.

It was Sunday evening, bright and summery. He was doing his homework and his mother was sitting on the carpet in one of her periodic fits of tidying out the drawers of the mahogany sideboard. On one side of her was a heap of paper scraps torn in quarters and bits of rubbish, on the other the useful items that had to be kept. The boy heard the bottom stair creak under Aunt Mary's light footstep. She knocked and put her head round the door and said that she was walking to Devotions. She was dressed in her good coat and hat and was just easing her fingers into her second glove. The boy saw her stop and pat her hair into place before the mirror in the hallway. Her mother stretched over and slammed the door shut. It vibrated, then he heard the deeper sound of the outside door closing and her first few steps on the gravelled driveway. He sat for a long time wondering if he would have time or not. Devotions could take anything from twenty minutes to three quarters of an hour, depending on who was saying it.

Ten minutes must have passed, then the boy left his homework and went upstairs and into his aunt's sitting room. He stood in front of the bureau wondering, then he reached for the keys. He tried several before he got the right one. The desk flap screeched as he pulled it down. He pretended to look at the postcards again in case there were any stamps he had missed. Then he put them away and reached for the bundle of letters. The elastic band was thick and old, brittle almost and when he took it off its track remained on the wad of letters. He carefully opened one and took out the letter and unfolded it, frail, khaki-coloured.

> My dearest Mary, it began. I am so tired I can hardly write
> to you. I have spent what seems like all day censoring
> letters (there is a howitzer about 100 yards away firing
> every 2 minutes). The letters are heartrending in their
> attempt to express what they cannot. Some of the men are
> illiterate, others almost so. I know that they feel as much
> as we do, yet they do not have the words to express it.
> That is your job in the schoolroom to give us generations
> who can read and write well. They have . . .

The boy's eye skipped down the page and over the next. He read the last paragraph.

> Mary I love you as much as ever – more so that we
> cannot be together. I do not know which is worse, the hurt
> of this war or being separated from you. Give all my love
> to Brendan and all at home.

It was signed, scribbled with what he took to be John. He folded the paper carefully into its original creases and put it in the envelope. He opened another.

> My love, it is thinking of you that keeps me sane. When I
> get a moment I open my memories of you as if I were
> reading. Your long dark hair – I always imagine you
> wearing the blouse with the tiny roses, the white one that
> opened down the back – your eyes that said so much

without words, the way you lowered your head when I said anything that embarrassed you, and the clean nape of your neck.

The day I think about most was the day we climbed the head at Ballycastle. In a hollow, out of the wind, the air full of pollen and the sound of insects, the grass warm and dry and you lying beside me with your hair undone, between me and the sun. You remember that that was where I kissed you and the look of disbelief in your eyes that made me laugh afterwards.

It makes me laugh now to see myself savouring these memories standing alone up to my thighs in muck. It is everywhere, two, three feet deep. To walk ten yards leaves you quite breathless.

I haven't time to write more today so I leave you with my feet in the clay and my head in the clouds. I love you,
John.

He did not bother to put the letter back in the envelope but opened another.

My dearest, I am so cold that I find it difficult to keep my hand steady enough to write. You remember when we swam the last two fingers of your hand went the colour and texture of candles with the cold. Well that is how I am all over. It is almost four days since I had any real sensation in my feet or legs. Everything is frozen. The ground is like steel.

Forgive me for telling you this but I feel I have to say it to someone. The worst thing is the dead. They sit or lie frozen in the position they died. You can distinguish them from the living because their faces are the colour of slate. God help us when the thaw comes . . . This war is beginning to have an effect on me. I have lost all sense of feeling. The only emotion I have experienced lately is one of anger. Sheer white trembling anger. I have no pity or sorrow for the dead and injured. I thank God it is not me but I am enraged that it has to be them. If I live through this experience I will be a different person.

The only thing that remains constant is my love for you.

Today a man died beside me. A piece of shrapnel had pierced his neck as we were moving under fire. I pulled him into a crater and stayed with him until he died. I

watched him choke and then drown in his blood.
I am full of anger which has no direction.

He sorted through the pile and read half of some, all of others.
The sun had fallen low in the sky and shone directly into the room
onto the pages he was reading making the paper glare. He
selected a letter from the back of the pile and shaded it with his
hand as he read.

Dearest Mary, I am writing this to you from my hospital
bed. I hope that you were not too worried about not
hearing from me. I have been here, so they tell me, for
two weeks and it took another two weeks before I could
bring myself to write this letter.
I have been thinking a lot as I lie here about the war
and about myself and about you. I do not know how to
say this but I feel deeply that I must do something, must
sacrifice something to make up for the horror of the past
year. In some strange way Christ has spoken to me
through the carnage . . .

Suddenly the boy heard the creak of the stair and he frantically
tried to slip the letter back into its envelope but it crumpled and
would not fit. He bundled them all together. He could hear his
aunt's familiar puffing on the short stairs to her room. He spread the
elastic band wide with his fingers. It snapped and the letters
scattered. He pushed them into their pigeon hole and quickly
closed the desk flap. The brass screeched loudly and clicked shut.
At that moment his aunt came into the room.
'What you are doing boy?' she snapped.
'Nothing.' He stood with the keys in his hand. She walked to the
bureau and opened it. The letters sprung out in an untidy heap.
'You have been reading my letters,' she said quietly. He mouth
was tight with the words and her eyes blazed. The boy could say
nothing. She struck him across the side of the face.
'Get out,' she said. 'Get out of my room.'
The boy, the side of his face stinging and red, put the keys on
the table on his way out. When he reached the door she called to
him. He stopped, his hand on the handle.
'You are dirt,' she hissed, 'and always will be dirt. I shall
remember this till the day I die.'

Even though it was a warm evening there was a fire in the large fireplace. His mother had asked him to light it so that she could clear out Aunt Mary's stuff. The room could then be his study, she said. She came in and seeing him at the table said, 'I hope I'm not disturbing you.'

'No.'

She took the keys from her pocket, opened the bureau and began burning papers and cards. She glanced quickly at each one before she flicked it onto the fire.

'Who was Brother Benignus?' he asked.

His mother stopped sorting and said, 'I don't know. Your aunt kept herself very much to herself. She got books from him through the post occasionally. That much I do know.'

She went on burning the cards. They built into strata, glowing red and black. Now and again she broke up the pile with the poker, sending showers of sparks up the chimney. He saw her come to the letters. She took off the elastic band and put it to one side with the useful things and began dealing the envelopes into the fire. She opened one and read quickly through it, then threw it on top of the burning pile.

'Mama,' he said.

'Yes?'

'Did Aunt Mary say anything about me?'

'What do you mean?'

'Before she died – did she say anything?'

'Not that I know of – the poor thing was too far gone to speak, God rest her.' She went on burning, lifting the corners of the letters with the poker to let the flames underneath them.

When he felt a hardness in his throat he put his head down on his books. Tears came into his eyes for the first time since she had died and he cried silently into the crook of his arm for the woman who had been his maiden aunt, his teller of tales, that she might forgive him.

devotions – prayers

Life in the trenches

The worst thing is the dead. They sit or lie frozen in the position they died.

I am writing this to you from my hospital bed. . .

Read

Study these photographs of life in the trenches and then read the poem which follows it.

The Death-bed

He drowsed and was aware of silence heaped
Round him, unshaken as the steadfast walls;
Aqueous like floating rays of amber light,
Soaring and quivering in the wings of sleep.
Silence and safety; and his mortal shore
Lipped by the inward, moonless waves of death.

Someone was holding water to his mouth.
He swallowed, unresisting; moaned and dropped
Through crimson gloom to darkness; and forgot
The opiate throb and ache that was his wound.
    Water – calm, sliding green above the weir.
    Water – a sky-lit alley for his boat,
    Bird-voiced, and bordered with reflected flowers
    And shaken hues of summer; drifting down,
    He dipped contented oars, and sighed, and slept.

Night, with a gust of wind, was in the ward,
Blowing the curtain to a glimmering curve.
Night. He was blind; he could not see the stars
Glinting among the wraiths of wandering cloud;
Queer blots of colour, purple, scarlet, green,
Flickered and faded in his drowning eyes.

Rain – he could hear it rustling through the dark;
Fragrance and passionless music woven as one;
Warm rain on drooping roses; pattering showers
That soak the woods; not the harsh rain that sweeps
Behind the thunder, but a trickling peace,
Gently and slowly washing life away.

                    *   *   *

He stirred, shifting his body; then the pain
Leapt like a prowling beast, and gripped and tore
His groping dreams with grinding claws and fangs.
    But someone was beside him; soon he lay
    Shuddering because that evil thing had passed.
    And death, who'd stepped toward him, paused and stared.

Light many lamps and gather round his bed.
Lend him your eyes, warm blood, and will to live.
Speak to him; rouse him; you may save him yet.
He's young; he hated War; how should he die
When cruel old campaigners win safe through?

But death replied: 'I choose him'. So he went,
And there was silence in the summer night;
Silence and safety; and the veils of sleep.
Then, far away, the thudding of the guns.

SIEGFRIED SASSOON

Talk

In pairs, discuss your reaction to the poem after one reading of it.

Make a list of:

(a) about six words from the poem that you would associate with life and young active people;

(b) about six words from the poem that remind you in some way of death or dying.

Read

Look up the meaning of any words in the poem that you do not understand.

Write

In pairs, after reading the poem more carefully, in a single sentence describe what you think is happening.

Talk

Which line in the poem do you think tells us most about what Siegfried Sassoon thought of young men killed in war? Explain your choice.

In what ways is the situation described in 'The Death-bed' similar to that experienced by John in *Secrets*?

Love in war

Read

Read these extracts from Vera Brittain's war diaries. Vera, like Mary in *Secrets*, has a boyfriend (Roland) who is fighting in the trenches.

April 19 1915

I had another violent fit of desperation this morning. I suppose I must get used to them, but they alarm me a little & make me wonder what I may do if Roland dies. At present my one desire in life is to see him again. I think how little hope there is of any tendency for the war to end, of how he is in the trenches day in and day out in momentary danger, of the long long weary months ahead, & I wonder how I shall ever bear them & get through them without any light, anything to look forward to, to carry me along. O glorious time of youth indeed! This is part of my life when I ought to be living every moment to the full, tasting the sweetness of every joy, full of love & life & aspiration and hope, exulting in my own existence. Instead, I can only think how weary are the heavy hours, wonder how I can get through their aching suspense, wonder when they will end – & how. Ah! those who are old & think this war so terrible do not know what it means to us who are young. They at least have had their joy, have it now to think of and look back on; for us the chief part of our lives, the part which makes all the rest worth while, has either never dawned, or else we have for a moment seen what is possible only to have it snatched from our eyes.

*   *   *

April 25 1915

. . . I wrote a long letter between lunch & tea telling him of my desire to nurse, of my wish that he should tell me of the horrors he sees because 'women are no longer the sheltered darlings of men's playtime, fit only for the nursery or the drawing-room.'

*   *   *

August 5 1915

. . . I received a letter from him before I went back to the hospital this evening . . . 'I used to talk of the Beauty of War, but it is only War in the abstract that is beautiful. Modern warfare is merely a trade, and it is only a matter of taste whether one is a soldier or a greengrocer, as far as I can see. Sometimes by dint of an opportunity a single man may rise from [the] sordidness to a deed of beauty, that is all.'

*   *   *

January 13 1916

I arrived at a very opportune though very awful moment. All R's things had just been sent back from the front and they were all lying on the floor. I had no idea before of the aftermath of an officer's death, or what the returned kit, about which so many letters have been written in the papers, really meant. It was terrible. Mrs Leighton and Clare were both crying as bitterly as on the day we heard of his death. There were his clothes – the clothes in which he came home from the front last time – another set rather less worn, and underclothing & accessories of various descriptions. Everything was damp & worn & simply caked with mud . . .

VERA BRITTAIN

Talk

In groups, discuss your reactions to these four diary entries. What do they tell us about the writer? Do you notice any changes in her attitudes?

Write

Look at the letters in *Secrets*. Allocate a letter to each person in your group: Imagine you were Mary receiving John's letters. Write a diary entry for the day you received his letter. Read all your diary extracts out loud, in the order that they would have happened.

Love letters

'You have been reading my letters,' she said quietly. Her mouth was tight with the words and her eyes blazed. The boy could say nothing. She struck him across the side of the face.

Read

During the First World War letters were the only means of communication between men at the Front and their loved ones. Often they were as much full of war as of love. Read these two extracts.

> 16 Middlesex Regiment,
> 29th Division,
> France.
> June 28th, 1916
>
> My darling Mother and Father,
> I am writing this on the eve of my first action. Tomorrow we go to the attack in the greatest battle the British Army has ever fought. I cannot quite express my feeling on this night and I cannot tell you if it is God's will that I shall come through but if I fall in battle then I shall have no regrets save for my loved ones I leave behind. It is a great cause and I came out willingly to serve my King and Country. My greatest concern is that I may have the courage and determination necessary to lead my platoon well.

> 26 September, 1915.
> My dear Maude
> I wonder if I shall ever finish this or if whether this morning is my last on earth. We have had a very terrible time during the last 24 hours and in half an hour have to make another attack with what I've got of my Battalion left with me, only just over 400. The rest are not all casualties though we've already had a good many. The men are scattered all over the place. After I had written to you yesterday we marched up to firing line, or rather just behind it and halted. From the reports which had come in it looked as if we should have an easy task before us. About 2pm my Brigade was ordered to reinforce which was said to have taken and were holding a hill called 70.

Talk

What attitudes to war do these letters display?

Assignment

Stage 1   Reread John's letters, especially the last one.

Stage 2   Imagine you were John. Make notes about what you think was happening to John during the period between the earliest letter and the postcards from Brother Benignus.

Stage 3   Plan this out carefully, using months and years to structure your thoughts.

Stage 4   Write three letters to Mary – one from the early part of the war, another from his hospital bed and the last from a much later period. Try to describe your feelings and thoughts as fully as you can, explaining any changes in your attitudes as realistically as you can. Include, also, some postcards that John might have sent Mary when he had become Brother Benignus later on.

Old people feel, too

Read

Read this article written by a sixty-year-old woman.

Love and sex are tricky for Little Old Ladies

FIRST PERSON

ARE you little, 60, and female?

If so, you qualify — as I have just done — as a Little Old Lady. Everyone who is younger (which seems to be most people) knows exactly what Little Old Ladies are like. For instance, it is well known that we're always in a muddle.

When we go to the supermarket we can never find what we want and we can never find an assistant who can tell us. So we spend a lot of time wandering about banging into other people's trollies. We then hold up the queue at the till while we fumble with plastic bags and get tangled up in the handles of our shopping-trollies. If we are trying to be really up to date and paying by cheque, the cheque-card will be under layers of pension-books, travel permits, cheap matinee tickets and various types of specs.

Our incompetence is known to be bottomless, indoors and out. If we attempt to knit we will drop about a quarter of our stitches, and turn out square purple garments everyone is too embarrassed to wear. If we venture on a short holiday, we are sure to be using last year's timetable, and the train we ask our children to meet no longer exists. And as we have no idea what a telephone card is, or where you'd get one, we can't ring from the station to tell them the train is tomorrow after all.

Indeed, the entire modern age is quite beyond the Little Old Lady. None of us could possible work a video, or even be quite sure what a video is. And if some kind of relation has given us a tape-recorder, we have no notion how to change the tape, or what to ask for when we need a new one. So the original tape eventually shreds into little bits which jam the machine, and it has to be hidden when the kind relation comes to stay.

So long as washing-machines are fairly basic we can be trusted with them, because they were around, in a primitive form, in the days when we were still young and competent. Even so, we must have the instructions handy, for the frequent consultation on which of the 24 electronic programmes we must use for what. Little Old Ladies have been heard to mutter that it would be simpler to do the washing in a river.

We can usually manage the basic knobs on the TV, and we're alright with the wireless so long as its got only long and medium wave. VHF and FM are, of course, quite beyond us and as for K. Hertz — we always thought that was a car hire-firm, or perhaps an American novelist.

Alcohol is known to be a problem area for Little Old Ladies. For a start, we're all suspected of being secret drinkers of cheap sherry. At a meal we're expected to prefer sweet white wine to vintage burgundy — and not much of that either. At parties we're asked if we'd prefer tomato juice. If we stand our ground, and go on repeating "Gin and Tonic" often enough, we will be given half a teaspoonful of gin in a quarter of a pint of tonic, because it's well known that we have weak heads.

And our public expects that because of our extreme old age we'll want to leave the party early. If we are still thought safe driving our own cars, we are sped away at 10.30 with anxious exhortations to drive carefully. If we have no car we are committed to the care of a cab-driver, and asked if we have enough money for the fare. Which brings me to the subject of driving. Whenever the car ahead is travelling at 20 miles an hour on the crown of the road; whenever someone opens a car-door in the path of your own advancing vehicle; whenever a car signalling left turns abruptly right under the bonnet of an advancing juggernaut — then you can be sure the driver is a Little Old Lady. And as everyone knows, we don't understand what the hard shoulder of a motorway is for, so we tend to use it for a little peaceful motoring when everyone else is going too fast.

Love and sex is another tricky area for Little Old Ladies. Clearly a Little Old Lady could never have fallen in love — and still less could anyone ever have fallen in love with her — because all Little Old Ladies are known to be semi-virginal, extremely ignorant, and very against sex. If she has had children, then obviously occasional sex has been forced upon her, but it's not considered suitable for her to refer to it.

She may be allowed to make occasional comments about the great Romantic moments of her life, but she mustn't do this too often, or with too much relish. At her age a Little Old Lady is certainly not expected to fall in love, because, in someone so old, falling in love is comic and embarrassing. She may be allowed to marry, if the arrangement seems suitable and convenient, and everyone is consulted, but things must not get soppy or out of hand.

It's thought to be quite sweet if she holds hands with her elderly gentleman friend, but that is definitely as far as things should go. If she wants any more than this, the Little Old Lady must draw her curtains or leave the country.

All Little Old Ladies are meant to enjoy coffee-mornings with other old folk. If we don't, we are definitely difficult and may have to go to a Home. A newly qualified Little Old Lady is used to being among the oldest in her household, then she suddenly finds, at the Old Folks' Coffee Morning, that she's a mere girl, a debutante.

In fact, all social life can be a problem for Little Old Ladies. unless we happen to catch a glimpse in a mirror, we can all too easily forget — in the general excitement of food and conversation — that we're old at all. A surprised look on the faces of our younger companions will remind us we're not playing the part expected. For instance, it's thought to be very tiresome for a Little Old Lady to actually know about anything. She must never be noisy or opinionated and is certainly not expected to have views on controversial topics such as Aids, or abortion, or the SDP (though she may, if she so wishes, express opinions on roses, soft furnishings, of the Queen's hats).

It is, of course, accepted that Little Old Ladies never know what the date is, always forget the shopping-list, can never remember the cost of second-class stamps, lose their specs a dozen times a day, and can't recollect either the title or the author of the book they have just put down. And because being old is so very tiring I must now take my afternoon rest. In fact, I'd better lie down before I forget what I came upstairs for.

Sheila Sullivan

Talk

In pairs, make a list of everything described by Sheila Sullivan as examples of things that older women are not meant to do or feel.

How does this humorous piece of writing help us to understand Mary in *Secrets*? How important are the memories she has of John to her in her old age? How much do you think her niece or great nephew understand her?

In groups, discuss which character you think is most important in this story and why.

Assignment

Stage 1   Interview an older member of your family or someone much older than yourself whom you know well. Prepare a list of questions beforehand. Ask them about their memories. Focus on important experiences, like significant relationships, or difficult times, such as war.

Stage 2   Use the information you find out to produce a feature on your chosen person for a local newspaper.

Unfulfilled love

The boy had noticed the ring when she read to him as a child . . . and her favourite extract, because she read it so often, Pip's meeting with Miss Havisham from *Great Expectations*

Read

Read this extract – the one Mary loved to read to her great-nephew.

I entered, therefore, and found myself in a pretty large room, well lighted with wax candles. No glimpse of daylight was to be seen in it. It was a dressing-room, and prominent in it was a draped table with a gilded looking-glass. In an armchair, with an elbow resting on the table and her head leaning on that hand, sat the strangest lady I have ever seen, or shall ever see.

She was dressed in rich materials – satins, and lace, and silks – all of white. Her shoes were white. And she had a long white veil dependent from her hair, and she had bridal flowers in her hair, but her hair was white. Some bright jewels sparkled on her neck and on her hands, and some other jewels lay sparkling on the table. Dresses, less splendid than the dress she wore, and half-packed trunks, were scattered about. She had not quite finished dressing, for she had but one shoe on – the other was on the table near her hand – her veil was but half arranged, her watch and chain were not put on, and some lace for her bosom lay with those trinkets, and with her handkerchief, and gloves, and some flowers, and a Prayer-book, all confusedly heaped about the looking-glass.

It was not in the first few moments that I saw all these things, though I saw more of them in the first moments than might be supposed. But, I saw that everything within my view which ought to be white, had been white long ago, and had lost its lustre, and was faded and yellow. I saw that the bride within the bridal dress had withered like the dress, and like the flowers, and had no brightness left but the brightness of her sunken eyes. I saw that the dress had been put upon the rounded figure of a young woman, and that the figure upon which it now hung loose, had shrunk to skin and bone.

'Who is it?' said the lady at the table.

'Pip, ma'am.'

'Pip?'

'Mr. Pumblechook's boy, ma'am. Come – to play.'

'Come nearer; let me look at you. Come close.'

It was when I stood before her, avoiding her eyes, that I took note of the surrounding objects in detail, and saw that her watch had stopped at twenty minutes to nine, and that a clock in the room had stopped at twenty minutes to nine.

'Look at me,' said Miss Havisham. 'You are not afraid of a woman who has never seen the sun since you were born?'

I regret to state that I was not afraid of telling the enormous lie comprehended in the answer 'No'.

'Do you know what I touch here?' she said, laying her hands, one upon the other, on her left side.

'Yes, ma'am.'

'What do I touch?'

'Your heart.'

'Broken!'

She uttered the word with an eager look, and with strong emphasis, and with a weird smile that had a kind of boast in it.

'I am tired,' said Miss Havisham. 'I want diversion, and I have done with men and women. Play. I sometimes have sick fancies,' she went on, 'and I have a sick fancy that I want to see some play. There, there!' with an impatient movement of the fingers of her right hand; 'play, play, play!'

I felt myself so unequal to the performance that I stood looking at Miss Havisham in what I suppose she took for a dogged manner, inasmuch as she said, when we had taken a good look at each other: 'Are you sullen and obstinate?'

'No, ma'am, I am very sorry for you, and very sorry I can't play just now. It's so new here, and so strange, and so fine – and melancholy—' I stopped, fearing I might say too much, or had already said it, and we took another look at each other.

CHARLES DICKENS

Talk

Make a list of all the similarities you can find between the situation of Mary and Miss Havisham. Why do you think Mary enjoyed reading it so much?

Mary's story

Assignment

Write a short story in which you describe some of the aspects of Mary's character hinted at in *Secrets*. You could set it in the War or later. You could retell *Secrets* from her point of view.

To Da-duh, In Memoriam

Paule Marshall

'. . . Oh Nana! all of you is not involved in this evil business Death,
Nor all of us in life.'
—From 'At My Grandmother's Grave,' by Lebert Bethune

I did not see her at first I remember. For not only was it dark inside
the crowded disembarkation shed in spite of the daylight flooding in
from outside, but standing there waiting for her with my mother and
sister I was still somewhat blinded from the sheen of tropical
sunlight on the water of the bay which we had just crossed in the
landing boat, leaving behind us the ship that had brought us from
New York lying in the offing. Besides, being only nine years of age
at the time and knowing nothing of islands I was busy attending to
the alien sights and sounds of Barbados, the unfamiliar smells.

I did not see her, but I was alerted to her approach by my
mother's hand which suddenly tightened around mine, and looking
up I traced her gaze through the gloom in the shed until I finally
made out the small, purposeful, painfully erect figure of the old
woman headed our way.

Her face was drowned in the shadow of an ugly rolled-brim brown
felt hat, but the details of her slight body and of the struggle taking
place within it were clear enough – an intense, unrelenting struggle
between her back which was beginning to bend ever so slightly
under the weight of her eighty-odd years and the rest of her which
sought to deny those years and hold that back straight, keep it in
line. Moving swiftly toward us (so swiftly it seemed she did not
intend stopping when she reached us but would sweep past us out
the doorway which opened onto the sea and like Christ walk upon
the water!), she was caught between the sunlight at her end of the
building and the darkness inside – and for a moment she appeared
to contain them both: the light in the long severe old-fashioned white
dress she wore which brought the sense of a past that was still
alive into our bustling present and in the snatch of white at her eye;
the darkness in her black high-top shoes and in her face which was
visible now that she was closer.

It was as stark and fleshless as a death mask, that face. The
maggots might have already done their work, leaving only the
framework of bone beneath the ruined skin and deep wells at the
temple and jaw. But her eyes were alive, unnervingly so for one so
old, with a sharp light that flicked out of the dim clouded depths like

a lizard's tongue to snap up all in her view. Those eyes betrayed a child's curiosity about the world, and I wondered vaguely seeing them, and seeing the way the bodice of her ancient dress had collapsed in on her flat chest (what had happened to her breasts?), whether she might not be some kind of child at the same time that she was a woman, with fourteen children, my mother included, to prove it. Perhaps she was both, both child and woman, darkness and light, past and present, life and death – all the opposites contained and reconciled in her.

'My Da-duh,' my mother said formally and stepped forward. The name sounded like thunder fading softly in the distance.

'Child,' Da-duh said, and her tone, her quick scrutiny of my mother, the brief embrace in which they appeared to shy from each other rather than touch, wiped out the fifteen years my mother had been away and restored the old relationship. My mother, who was such a formidable figure in my eyes, had suddenly with a word been reduced to my status.

'Yes, God is good,' Da-duh said with a nod that was like a tic. 'He has spared me to see my child again.'

We were led forward then, apologetically because not only did Da-duh prefer boys but she also liked her grandchildren to be 'white,' that is, fair-skinned; and we had, I was to discover, a number of cousins, the outside children of white estate managers and the like, who qualified. We, though, were as black as she.

My sister being the oldest was presented first. 'This one takes after the father,' my mother said and waited to be reproved.

Frowning, Da-duh tilted my sister's face toward the light. But her frown soon gave way to a grudging smile, for my sister with her large mild eyes and little broad winged nose, with our father's high-cheeked Barbadian cast to her face, was pretty.

'She's goin' be lucky,' Da-duh said and patted her once on the cheek. 'Any girl child that takes after the father does be lucky.'

She turned then to me. But oddly enough she did not touch me. Instead leaning close, she peered hard at me, and then quickly drew back. I thought I saw her hand start up as though to shield her eyes. It was almost as if she saw not only me, a thin truculent child who it was said took after no one but myself, but something in me which for some reason she found disturbing, even threatening. We looked silently at each other for a long time there in the noisy shed, our gaze locked. She was the first to look away.

'But Adry,' she said to my mother and her laugh was cracked, thin, apprehensive. 'Where did you get this one here with this fierce look?'

'We don't know where she came out of, my Da-duh,' my mother said, laughing also. Even I smiled to myself. After all I had won the encounter. Da-duh had recognized my small strength – and this was all I ever asked of the adults in my life then.

'Come, soul,' Da-duh said and took my hand. 'You must be one of those New York terrors you hear so much about.'

She led us, me at her side and my sister and mother behind, out of the shed into the sunlight that was like a bright driving summer rain and over to a group of people clustered beside a decrepit lorry. They were our relatives, most of them from St. Andrews although Da-duh herself lived in St. Thomas, the women wearing bright print dresses, the colors vivid against their darkness, the men rusty black suits that encased them like straight-jackets. Da-duh, holding fast to my hand, became my anchor as they circled round us like a nervous sea, exclaiming, touching us with their calloused hands, embracing us shyly. They laughed in awed bursts: 'But look Adry got big-big children!' / 'And see the nice things they wearing, wrist watch and all!' / 'I tell you, Adry has done all right for sheself in New York . . .'

Da-duh, ashamed at their wonder, embarrassed for them, admonished them the while. 'But oh Christ,' she said, 'why you all got to get on like you never saw people from "Away" before? You would think New York is the only place in the world to hear wunna. That's why I don't like to go anyplace with you St. Andrews people, you know. You all ain't been colonized.'

We were in the back of the lorry finally, packed in among the barrels of ham, flour, cornmeal and rice and the trunks of clothes that my mother had brought as gifts. We made our way slowly through Bridgetown's clogged streets, part of a funereal procession of cars and open-sided buses, bicycles and donkey carts. The dim little limestone shops and offices along the way marched with us, at the same mournful pace, toward the same grave ceremony – as did the people, the women balancing huge baskets on top of their heads as if they were no more than hats they wore to shade them from the sun. Looking over the edge of the lorry I watched as their feet slurred the dust. I listened and their voices, raw and loud and dissonant in the heat, seemed to be grappling with each other high overhead.

Da-duh sat on a trunk in our midst, a monarch amid her court. She still held my hand, but it was different now. I had suddenly become her anchor, for I felt her fear of the lorry with its asthmatic motor (a fear and distrust, I later learned, she held of all machines) beating like a pulse in her rough palm.

As soon as we left Bridgetown behind though, she relaxed, and while the others around us talked she gazed at the canes standing tall on either side of the winding marl road. 'C'dear', she said softly to herself after a time. 'The canes this side are pretty enough.'

They were too much for me. I thought of them as giant weeds that had overrun the island, leaving scarcely any room for the small tottering houses of sunbleached pine we passed or the people, dark streaks as our lorry hurtled by. I suddenly feared that we were journeying, unaware that we were, toward some dangerous place where the canes, grown as high and thick as a forest, would close in on us and run us through with their stiletto blades. I longed then for the familiar: for the street in Brooklyn where I lived, for my father who had refused to accompany us ('Blowing out good money on foolishness,' he had said of the trip), for a game of tag with my friends under the chestnut tree outside our aging brownstone house.

'Yes, but wait till you see St. Thomas canes,' Da-duh was saying to me. 'They's canes father, bo,' she gave a proud arrogant nod. 'Tomorrow, God willing, I goin' take you out in the ground and show them to you.'

True to her word Da-duh took me with her the following day out into the ground. It was a fairly large plot adjoining her weathered board and shingle house and consisting of a small orchard, a good-sized canepiece and behind the canes, where the land sloped abruptly down, a gully. She had purchased it with Panama money sent her by her eldest son, my uncle Joseph, who had died working on the canal. We entered the ground along a trail no wider than her body and as devious and complex as her reasons for showing me her land. Da-duh strode briskly ahead, her slight form filled out this morning by the layers of sacking petticoats she wore under her working dress to protect her against the damp. A fresh white cloth, elaborately arranged around her head, added to her height, and lent her a vain, almost roguish air.

Her pace slowed once we reached the orchard, and glancing back at me occasionally over her shoulder, she pointed out the various trees.

'This here is a breadfruit,' she said. 'That one yonder is a papaw. Here's a guava. This is a mango. I know you don't have anything like these in New York. Here's a sugar apple.' (The fruit looked more like artichokes than apples to me.) 'This one bears limes . . .' She went on for some time, intoning the names of the trees as though they were those of her gods. Finally, turning to me, she said, 'I know you don't have anything this nice where you come from.' Then, as I hesitated: 'I said I known you don't have anything this nice where you come from . . .'

'No,' I said and my world did seem suddenly lacking.

Da-duh nodded and passed on. The orchard ended and we were on the narrow cart road that led through the canepiece, the canes clashing like swords above my cowering head. Again she turned and her thin muscular arms spread wide, her dim gaze embracing the small field of canes, she said – and her voice almost broke under the weight of her pride, 'Tell me, have you got anything like these in that place where you were born?'

'No.'

'I din' think so. I bet you don't even know that these canes here and the sugar you eat is one and the same thing. That they does throw the canes into some damn machine at the factory and squeeze out all the little life in them to make sugar for you all so in New York to eat. I bet you don't know that.'

'I've got two cavities and I'm not allowed to eat a lot of sugar.'

But Da-duh didn't hear me. She had turned with an inexplicably angry motion and was making her way rapidly out of the canes and down the slope at the edge of the field which led to the gully below. Following her apprehensively down the incline amid a stand of banana plants whose leaves flapped like elephants' ears in the wind, I found myself in the middle of a small tropical wood – a place dense and damp and gloomy and tremulous with the fitful play of light and shadow as the leaves high above moved against the sun that was almost hidden from view. It was a violent place, the tangled foliage fighting each other for a chance at the sunlight, the branches of the trees locked in what seemed an immemorial struggle, one both necessary and inevitable. But despite the violence, it was pleasant, almost peaceful in the gully, and beneath the thick undergrowth the earth smelled like spring.

This time Da-duh didn't even bother to ask her usual question, but simply turned and waited for me to speak.

'No,' I said, my head bowed. 'We don't have anything like this in New York.'

'Ah,' she cried, her triumph complete. 'I din' think so. Why, I've heard that's a place where you can walk till you near drop and never see a tree.'

'We've got a chestnut tree in front of our house,' I said.

'Does it bear?' She waited. 'I ask you, does it bear?'

'Not anymore,' I muttered. 'It used to, but not anymore.'

She gave the nod that was like a nervous twitch. 'You see,' she said. 'Nothing can bear there.' Then, secure behind her scorn, she added, 'But tell me, what's this snow like that you hear so much about?'

Looking up, I studied her closely, sensing my chance, and then I told her, describing at length and with as much drama as I could summon not only what snow in the city was like, but what it would be like here, in her perennial summer kingdom.

'. . . And you see all these trees you got here,' I said. 'Well, they'd be bare. No leaves, no fruit, nothing. They'd be covered in snow. You see your canes. They'd be buried under tons of snow. The snow would be higher than your head, higher than your house, and you wouldn't be able to come down into this here gully because it would be snowed under. . . .'

She searched my face for the lie, still scornful but intrigued. 'What a thing, huh?' she said finally, whispering it softly to herself.

'And when it snows you couldn't dress like you are now,' I said. 'Oh no, you'd freeze to death. You'd have to wear a hat and gloves and galoshes and ear muffs so your ears wouldn't freeze and drop off, and a heavy coat. I've got a Shirley Temple coat with fur on the collar. I can dance. You wanna see?'

Before she could answer I began, with a dance called the Truck which was popular back then in the 1930's. My right forefinger waving, I trucked around the nearby trees and around Da-duh's awed and rigid form. After the Truck I did the Suzy-Q, my lean hips swishing, my sneakers sidling zigzag over the ground. 'I can sing,' I said and did so, starting with 'I'm Gonna Sit Right Down and Write Myself a Letter,' then without pausing, 'Tea For Two,' and ending with 'I Found a Million Dollar Baby in a Five and Ten Cent Store.'

For long moments afterwards Da-duh stared at me as if I were a creature from Mars, an emissary from some world she did not know but which intrigued her and whose power she both felt and feared. Yet something about my performance must have pleased her, because bending down she slowly lifted her long skirt and then, one by one, the layers of petticoats until she came to a drawstring purse dangling at the end of a long strip of cloth tied round her waist. Opening the purse she handed me a penny. 'Here,' she said half-smiling against her will. 'Take this to buy yourself a sweet at the shop up the road. There's nothing to be done with you, soul.'

From then on, whenever I wasn't taken to visit relatives, I accompanied Da-duh out into the ground, and alone with her amid the canes or down in the gully I told her about New York. It always began with some slighting remark on her part: 'I know they don't have anything this nice where you come from,' or 'Tell me I hear those foolish people in New York does do such and such. . . . ' But as I answered, recreating my towering world of steel and concrete and machines for her, building the city out of words, I would feel her give way. I came to know the signs of her surrender: the total stillness that would come over her little hard dry form, the probing gaze that like a surgeon's knife sought to cut through my skull to get at the images there, to see if I were lying; above all, her fear, a fear nameless and profound, the same one I had felt beating in the palm of her hand that day in the lorry.

Over the weeks I told her about refrigerators, radios, gas stoves, elevators, trolley cars, wringer washing machines, movies, airplanes, the cyclone at Coney Island, subways, toasters, electric lights: 'At night, see, all you have to do is flip this little switch on the wall and all the lights in the house go on. Just like that. Like magic. It's like turning on the sun at night.'

'But tell me,' she said to me once with a faint mocking smile, 'do the white people have all these things too or it's only the people looking like us?'

I laughed. 'What d'ya mean,' I said. 'The white people have even better.' Then: 'I beat up a white girl in my class last term.'

'Beating up white people!' Her tone was incredulous.

'How you mean!' I said, using an expression of hers. 'She called me a name.'

For some reason Da-duh could not quite get over this and repeated in the same hushed, shocked voice, 'beating up white people now! Oh, the lord, the world's changing up so I can scarce recognize it anymore.'

One morning towards the end of our stay, Da-duh led me into a part of the gully that we had never visited before, an area darker and more thickly overgrown than the rest, almost impenetrable. There in a small clearing amid the dense bush, she stopped before an incredibly tall royal palm which rose cleanly out of the ground, and drawing the eye up with it, soared high above the trees around it into the sky. It appeared to be touching the blue dome of sky, to be flaunting its dark crown of fronds right in the blinding white face of the late morning sun.

Da-duh watched me a long time before she spoke, and then she said, very quietly, 'All right, now, tell me if you've got anything this tall in that place you're from.'

I almost wished, seeing her face, that I could have said no.

'Yes,' I said. 'We've got buildings hundreds of times this tall in New York. There's one called the Empire State building that's the tallest in the world. My class visited it last year and I went all the way to the top. It's got over a hundred floors. I can't describe how tall it is. Wait a minute. What's the name of that hill I went to visit the other day, where they have the police station?'

'You mean Bissex?'

'Yes, Bissex. Well, the Empire State Building is way taller than that.'

'You're lying now!' she shouted, trembling with rage. Her hand lifted to strike me.

'No, I'm not,' I said. 'It really is, if you don't believe me I'll send you a picture postcard of it soon as I get back home so you can see for yourself. But it's way taller than Bissex.'

All the fight went out of her at that. The hand poised to strike me fell limp to her side, and as she stared at me, seeing not me but the building that was taller than the highest hill she knew, the small stubborn light in her eyes (it was the same amber as the flame in the kerosene lamp she lit at dusk) began to fail. Finally, with a vague gesture that even in the midst of her defeat still tried to dismiss me and my world, she turned and started back through the gully, walking slowly, her steps groping and uncertain, as if she were suddenly no longer sure of the way, while I followed triumphant yet strangely saddened behind.

The next morning I found her dressed for our morning walk but stretched out on the Berbice chair in the tiny drawing room where she sometimes napped during the afternoon heat, her face turned to the window beside her. She appeared thinner and suddenly indescribably old.

'My Da-duh,' I said.

'Yes, nuh,' she said. Her voice was listless and the face she slowly turned my way was, now that I think back on it, like a Benin mask, the features drawn and almost distorted by an ancient abstract sorrow.

'Don't you feel well?' I asked.

'Girl, I don't know.'

'My Da-duh, I goin' boil you some bush tea,' my aunt, Da-duh's youngest child, who lived with her, called from the shed roof kitchen.

'Who tell you I need bush tea?' she cried, her voice assuming for a moment its old authority. 'You can't even rest nowadays without some malicious person looking for you to be dead. Come girl,' she motioned me to a place beside her on the old-fashioned lounge chair, 'give us a tune.'

I sang for her until breakfast at eleven, all my brash irreverent Tin Pan Alley songs, and then just before noon we went out into the ground. But it was a short, dispirited walk. Da-duh didn't even notice that the mangoes were beginning to ripen and would have to be picked before the village boys got to them. And when she paused occasionally and looked out across the canes or up at her trees it wasn't as if she were seeing them but something else. Some huge, monolithic shape had imposed itself, it seemed, between her and the land, obstructing her vision. Returning to the house she slept the entire afternoon on the Berbice chair.

She remained like this until we left, languishing away the mornings on the chair at the window gazing out at the land as if it were already doomed; then, at noon, taking the brief stroll with me through the ground during which she seldom spoke, and afterwards returning home to sleep till almost dusk sometimes.

On the day of our departure she put on the austere, ankle length white dress, the black shoes and brown felt hat (her town clothes she called them), but she did not go with us to town. She saw us off on the road outside her house and in the midst of my mother's tearful protracted farewell, she leaned down and whispered in my ear, 'Girl, you're not to forget now to send me the picture of that building, you hear.'

By the time I mailed her the large colored picture postcard of the Empire State building she was dead. She died during the famous '37 strike which began shortly after we left. On the day of her death England sent planes flying low over the island in a show of force – so low, according to my aunt's letter, that the downdraft from them shook the ripened mangoes from the trees in Da-duh's orchard. Frightened, everyone in the village fled into the canes. Except Da-duh. She remained in the house at the window so my aunt said, watching as the planes came swooping and screaming like monstrous birds down over the village, over her house, rattling her trees and flattening the young canes in her field. It must have seemed to her lying there that they did not intend pulling out of their dive, but like the hardback beetles which hurled themselves with suicidal force against the walls of the house at night, those menacing silver shapes would hurl themselves in an ecstasy of self-immolation onto the land, destroying it utterly.

When the planes finally left and the villagers returned they found her dead on the Berbice chair at the window.

She died and I lived, but always, to this day even, within the shadow of her death. For a brief period after I was grown I went to live alone, like one doing penance, in a loft above a noisy factory in downtown New York and there painted seas of sugar-cane and huge swirling Van Gogh suns and palm trees striding like brightly-plumed Tutsi warriors across a tropical landscape, while the thunderous tread of the machines downstairs jarred the floor beneath my easel, mocking my efforts.

Berbice chair – a relaxing chair
bush tea – green tea, made with young leaves

Emigration from Barbados

Read

During the twentieth century, West Indian people emigrated to many
countries, including Venezuela, Panama, Honduras, the USA (New
York in particular) and, especially after 1945, to Britain. Some of Da-
Duh's family had moved to New York during the 1920s. Study this
map and photograph to give you an idea of the background of *To Da-
Duh*.

*This map shows the movement of people from Barbados and other West Indian
islands to the United States*

Barbadian emigrants arrive at their new home

Changing the political climate

She died during the famous '37 strike which began shortly after we left. On the day of her death England sent planes flying low over the island in a show of force. . .

Read

During the period in which this story is set and immediately after the Second World War, many of the Caribbean islands began to want independent rule. For Barbados, a British colony, 1937 was an important year in which working class people began to assert their independence. Read this description of changing attitudes.

Barbados was still dominated by the planter class. In business, social life and politics the large plantation owners and merchants of Bridgetown held sway. There were some coloured members in the Assembly, but up until 1937 they made little impact.

In March of that year a man called Clement Payne arrived in Barbados from Trinidad. He was the son of Barbadian parents, but had been born in Trinidad. There he had picked up ideas on workers' organisations and strike action. As soon as he arrived in Barbados he began to hold meetings at which he urged Barbadians to organise themselves in protest against their poverty and unemployment. He was a fiery orator and the size of his audience grew larger and larger. This raised fears among the authorities and a way was soon found to silence Clement Payne; when he had arrived in Bridgetown from Trinidad Payne had told the immigration officials that he had been born in Barbados, and he was now charged with having made a false statement and wilfully lying about his place of birth. Amidst wide-spread protest from his followers in Barbados, Payne was found guilty. He appealed and was defended by a successful young lawyer, Grantley Adams. The case was quashed, but an order was issued for Payne to be deported and Adams was unable to prevent this.

When his supporters learnt that Payne had been put aboard a steamship without their knowledge their anger overflowed. They swept through Bridgetown in disorganised mobs, smashing motor cars, shop windows and street lamps. They showered the police with bottles and stones and as the news spread into the countryside hungry estate workers raided potato fields. British warships were summoned to restore order and the police were ordered to use their guns. Fourteen people were killed, 47 wounded and over 400 were arrested.

The shock of these riots stunned Barbados. The society could no longer quietly accept the poverty in its midst. An official Commission of Enquiry pointed to the root cause of the trouble as being poverty and unemployment. The Colonial Office pushed the local government to correct the imbalances by providing workmen's compensation, old age pensions, minimum wages and enacting trade union laws.

LENNOX HONYCHURCH, *THE CARIBBEAN PEOPLE* BOOK 3

Talk

In groups, talk about:

● what you think Da-Duh thought about people who emigrated from Barbados;
● how you think she might have reacted to the protest organised by Clement Payne.

Do you think that Paule's mother would have reacted in the same way as Da-duh to the changes on Barbados? Explain your reasons.

Assignment

Expand on what you imagine took place on the day of the meeting between Da-Duh and her grand-daughter. Write two diary entries, one for a page from Da-Duh's diary, one for her grand-daughter's.

● Remember to show their different ages and different ways of speaking and thinking.
● Think carefully about what each might have chosen to write about this important first meeting.

Visiting your past

Read

Read what Paule Marshall wrote about the subject of this story.

This is the most autobiographical of the stories, a reminiscence largely of a visit I paid to my grandmother (whose nickname was Da-Duh) on the island of Barbados when I was nine. Ours was a complex relationship – close, affectionate yet rivalrous. During the year I spent with her a subtle kind of power struggle went on between us. It was as if we both knew, at a level beyond words, that I had come into the world not only to love and to continue her line but to take her very life in order that I might live.

Talk

In pairs, talk about what you think Paule Marshall means by the last sentence of her comment about the story. Make a list of all the possible ways in which you could imagine that it might have been necessary for an old woman to die so that her young grandchild could live.

Paule Marshall

Returning to Jamaica

Read

Read this account which was written by a school student about a visit
to another Caribbean island.

We arrived at the airport hungry and tired from the flight and we
were greeted by my family who reside in Jamaica. The first person
to greet us was my grandmother in whose house we would be
staying. She's a tall lady, heavily-built with broad shoulders. She
nearly always wears a black and white dress with no sleeves. Her
favourite black shawl hung from her shoulders. There was a smell of
wild flowers around her, as if she was wearing a new perfume. The
other members of the family greeted us in turn. Grandfather and my
other uncles were all dressed in their best suits.

As we crossed the dirty street we passed through a little town. The
sweet smell of West-Indian cooking entered our nostrils. Sheer
Delight! The smell of sweetcorn and rice rising up through the
streets mixed with that of the heavy dust atmosphere was
overpoweringly intoxicating.

We approached the family house belonging to my grandfather. The
white stone work shone brilliantly like a shiny new pin. It was a very
big house, one of the biggest in the street. My grandfather had
bought it the last time he had come to Jamaica. He runs a night-club
in Britain which is doing very well. He tends to think of himself as a
'cool dude'. I personally think he acts a bit too young for his age but
if that's what he wants to do then let him. His usual wear is a baggy
suit, white socks a tie and a hat.

Unpacking completed, we went downstairs to grab some lunch.
We were famished, but what greeted us was not a normal person's
shock, but a full-sized feast for about seven people. Several smells
filled my nostrils. The overpowering smell of spiced curry and lamb
was the first smell that hit me.

Reaching the table I saw a great variety of colours. Reds, yellows,
greens, dark browns and light browns. Pepper and chillies cut into
perfect little cubes and added to the sweetcorn to make a better
dish. The centre of the table held a vase of fesh flowers which
smelled of the fragrance of a beautiful hillside of flowers after the
morning dew. There were small red daisy-shaped flowers and larger
dahlia blue flowers.

Next to the flowers was a bowl full to overflowing with the most
beautiful fruit and vegetables I have ever seen. And upon each
vegetable not a spot was to be found. Yellow bunches of bananas
hung from the ceiling above the table in a hanging fruitbowl. Green
bananas decorated the table on a dish in an eight-pointed star
shape.

In Jamaica green bananas are grilled or fried and then the skin is
removed and the soft flesh of the banana is left. This is then cooked
with honey or a sauce and then the banana is placed back into its
half-open peel.

This has been my favourite holiday of all time, meeting new relations and making new friends, tasting new mouth-watering dishes and experiencing the warmth, friendship and openness of the whole community.

RODERIQUE CAMPBELL-EVANS

Talk

In groups make a list of the ways in which this piece of writing is similar to the story by Paule Marshall. In what ways are the two passages different?

Grandparents

Her face was drowned in the shadow of an ugly rolled-brim brown felt hat . . . Perhaps she was both, both child and woman, darkness and light, past and present, life and death – all the opposites contained and reconciled in her.

Talk

In groups, describe your own grandparents or any memories you may have of older members of your own family who you have only seen occasionally. You may find it helpful to reread Paule Marshall's strong description of her grandmother in the first few pages of the story.

Describe all that you know about the place where your mother and father were born. What does it mean to you? Have you visited it? Explain your thoughts and any feelings you may have about these places.

How much do you know about where your grandparents were born and where they lived?

Read

Read these two poems written by grand-daughters about their grandmothers. The first is by a well-known poet, Elizabeth Jennings. The second was written by a sixteen-year-old school student, Sonia Pearce. After it are some of Sonia's own comments on the circumstances surrounding the writing of the poem.

My Grandmother

She kept an antique shop – or it kept her.
Among Apostle spoons and Bristol glass,
The faded silks, the heavy furniture,
She watched her own reflection in the brass
Salvers and silver bowls, as if to prove
Polish was all, there was no need of love.

And I remember how I once refused
To go out with her, since I was afraid.
It was perhaps a wish not to be used
Like antique objects. Though she never said
That she was hurt, I still could feel the guilt
Of that refusal, guessing how she felt.

Later, too frail to keep a shop, she put
All her best things in one long narrow room.
The place smelt old, of things too long kept shut,
The smell of absences where shadows come
That can't be polished. There was nothing then
To give her own reflection back again.

And when she died I felt no grief at all,
Only the guilt of what I once refused.
I walked into her room among the tall
Sideboards and cupboards – things she never used
But needed: and no finger-marks were there,
Only the new dust falling through the air.

ELIZABETH JENNINGS

Grandmother

She's dead.
The words put a sudden stop to one of my inner thoughts
And already new thoughts planted themselves
And started growing.
A part of me wanted to yell out and ask for my Grandmother back.

But ask who?
What right had I? I was only an intruder.
That fact of life caused the most pain,
A secret pain that no one will ever seek out its hiding place.

Was this my part for mourning?
My father, the son,
My mother, the daughter-in-law,
And me. Which character did I play?
I had passed her life as a complete stranger.
And I blame time for this.
For my Grandmother, time was long enough.
For me, it was too short.

SONIA PEARCE

I wrote this poem a few weeks after my grandmother died. It was written through anger, an anger that I can only express through writing. The fact was that my Mum and I were planning to go and see her at the end of the year. During the time I used to wonder, would I ever get to Jamaica to see her? What did she look like? Would I like her?

My grandmother knew my father, and my mother, and she met my sister, but, though she played a part in my life, we never got to know each other, not even through letters. We were strangers, and that was what hurt me most. I got confused over whether to miss her or not, because in one way her death could have affected me as little as the death of a stranger in the street. Your feelings are decided by how much you know the person.

SONIA PEARCE

Talk

In pairs, make a list of all the words you would use to describe the two grandmothers in these poems.

In groups, discuss:

● the different attitudes to the death of a grandparent shown in the two poems;
● what it is that the poet remembers about her grandmother;
● what is special about the relationship described.

Assignment

Choose an older member of your own close family who is or was important to you. Write a story about your relationship and include an important meeting or period where you spent time with this person. Try to describe what the relationship meant and/or means to you.

The power struggle

Write

Paule Marshall describes her relationship with her grandmother as a kind of power struggle between old and young. Study these quotations from the story and then, in pairs:

● put them in order;
● write brief notes about what each one tells the reader about their relationship.

A   She died and I lived, but always, to this day even, within the shadow of her death.

B   . . . her face which was visible now that she was closer. It was as stark as a death mask, that face. The maggots might have already done their work . . .

C   'Where did you get this one here with this fierce look?'

D   She turned then to me. But oddly enough she did not touch me.

E   She still held my hand but it was different now.

F   'You must be one of those New York terrors you hear so much about.'

G   'Tomorrow, God willing, I goin' take you out in the ground and show them to you.'

H   'Take this to buy yourself a sweet at the shop up the road. There's nothing to be done with you soul.'

I   'I'll send you a postcard of it soon as I get back home so you can see for yourself.'

J   I almost wished, seeing her face, that I could have said no.

K   'My Da-Duh,' I said.

L   'Come girl,' she motioned me to a place beside her on the old-fashioned lounge chair, 'give us a tune.'

Assignment

Write an essay about how the relationship between Paule Marshall and Da-Duh is developed in this story. Include quotations selected from the ones you have just been discussing and any that you chose yourself. Try and go into as much detail as you can at all stages of your essay. In particular, give examples whenever you are attempting to describe a new phase in their development.

The Badness Within Him

Susan Hill

The night before, he had knelt beside his bed and prayed for a storm, an urgent, hysterical prayer. But even while he prayed he had known that there could be no answer, because of the badness within him, a badness which was living and growing like a cancer. So that he was not surprised to draw back the curtains and see the pale, glittering mist of another hot day. But he was angry. He did not want the sun and the endless stillness and brightness, the hard-edged shadows and the steely gleam of the sea. They came to this place every summer, they had been here, now, since the first of August, and they had one week more left. The sun had shone from the beginning. He wondered how he would bear it.

At the breakfast table, Jess sat opposite to him and her hand kept moving up to rub at the sunburned skin which was peeling off her nose.

'Stop *doing* that.'

Jess looked up slowly. This year, for the first time, Col felt the difference in age between them, he saw that Jess was changing, moving away from him to join the adults. She was almost fourteen.

'What if the skin doesn't grow again? What then? You look awful enough now.'

She did not reply, only considered him for a long time, before returning her attention to the cereal plate. After a moment, her hand went up again to the peeling skin.

Col thought, I hate it here. I hate it. *I hate it.* And he clenched his fist under cover of the table until the fingernails hurt him, digging into his palm. He had suddenly come to hate it, and the emotion frightened him. It was the reason why he had prayed for the storm, to break the pattern of long, hot, still days and waken the others out of their contentment, to change things. Now, everything was as it had always been in the past and he did not want the past, he wanted the future.

But the others were happy here, they slipped into the gentle lazy routine of summer as their feet slipped into sandals, they never grew bored or angry or irritable, never quarrelled with one another. For days now Col had wanted to quarrel.

How had he ever been able to bear it? And he cast about, in his frustration, for some terrible event, as he felt the misery welling up inside him at the beginning of another day.

I hate it here. He hated the house itself, the chintz curtains and

covers bleached by the glare of the sun, and the crunch of sand
like sugar spilled in the hall and along the tiled passages, the
windows with peeling paint always open on to the garden, and the
porch cluttered with sandshoes and buckets and deckchairs, the
muddle and shabbiness of it all.

They all came down to breakfast at different times, and ate slowly
and talked of nothing, made no plans, for that was what the holiday
was for, a respite from plans and time-tables.

Fay pulled out the high chair and sat her baby down next to Col.

'You can help him with his egg.'

'Do I have to?'

Fay stared at him, shocked that anyone should not find her child
desirable.

'Do help, Col, you know the baby can't manage by himself.'

'Col's got a black dog on his shoulder.'

'Shut up.'

'A perfectly enormous, coal black, monster of a dog!'

He kicked out viciously at his sister under the table. Jess began
to cry.

'Now, Col, you are to apologize please.' His mother looked paler
than ever, exhausted. Fay's baby dug fingers of toast down deeper
and deeper into the yolk of egg.

'You hurt me, you hurt me.'

He looked out of the window. The sea was a thin, glistening line.
Nothing moved. Today would be the same as yesterday and all the
other days – nothing would happen, nothing would change. He felt
himself itching beneath his skin.

They had first come here when he was three years old. He
remembered how great the distance had seemed as he jumped
from rock to rock on the beach, how he had scarcely been able to
stretch his leg across and balance. Then, he had stood for minute
after minute feeling the damp ribs of sand under his feet. He had
been enchanted with everything. He and Jess had collected
buckets full of sea creatures from the rock pools and put them into
a glass aquarium in the scullery, though always the starfish and
anemones and limpets died after a few, captive days. They had
taken jam jars up on to West Cliff and walked along, at the hottest
part of the day, looking for chrysalis on the grass stalks. The salt
had dried in white tide marks around their brown legs, and Col had
reached down and rubbed some off with his finger and then licked
it. In the sun lounge the moths and butterflies had swollen and
cracked open their frail, papery coverings and crept out like babies
from the womb, and he and Jess had sat up half the night by the

light of moon or candle, watching them.

And so it had been every year and often, in winter or windy spring in London, he remembered it all, the smell of the sunlit house and the feeling of the warm sea lapping against his thighs and the line of damp woollen bathing shorts outside the open back door. It was another world, but it was still there, and when summer came they would return to it, things would be the same.

Yet now, he wanted to do some violence in this house, he wanted an end to everything. He was afraid of himself.

'Col's got a black dog on his shoulder!'

So he left them and went for a walk on his own, over the track beside the gorse bushes and up on to the coarse grass of the sheep field behind West Cliff. The mist was rolling away, the sea was white-gold at the edges, creaming back. On the far side of the field there were poppies.

He lay down and pressed his face and hands into the warm turf until he could smell the soil beneath and gradually, he felt the warmth of the sun on his back and it soothed him.

In the house, his mother and sisters left the breakfast table and wandered upstairs to find towels and sunhats and books, content that this day should be the same as all the other days, wanting the summer to last. And later, his father would join them for the weekend, coming down on the train from London, he would discard the blue city suit and emerge, hairy and thickly fleshed, to lie on a rug and snore and play with Fay's baby, rounding off the family circle.

By eleven it was hotter than it had been all summer, the dust rose in soft clouds when a car passed down the lane to the village, and did not settle again, and the leaves of the hedge were mottled and dark, the birds went quiet. Col felt his own anger like a pain tightening around his head. He went up to the house and lay on his bed trying to read, but the room was airless and the sunlight fell in a straight, hard beam across his bed and on to the printed page, making his eyes hurt.

When he was younger he had liked this room, he had sometimes dreamed of it when he was in London. He had collected shells and small pebbles and laid them out in careful piles, and hung up a bladder-wrack on a nail by the open window, had brought books from home about fossils and shipwrecks and propped them on top of the painted wooden chest. But now it felt too small, it stifled him, it was a childish room, a pale, dead room in which nothing ever happened and nothing would change.

After a while he heard his father's taxi come up the drive.

'Col, do watch what you're doing near the baby, you'll get sand in his eyes.'

'Col, if you want to play this game with us, do, but otherwise go away, if you can't keep still, you're just spoiling it.'

'Col, why don't you build a sandcastle or something?'

He stood looking down at them all, at his mother and Fay playing cards in the shade of the green parasol, and his father lying on his back, his bare, black-haired chest shiny with oil and his nostrils flaring in and out as he breathed, at Jess, who had begun to build a sandcastle for the baby, instead of him. She had her hair tied back in bunches and the freckles had come out even more thickly across her cheekbones, she might have been eleven years old. But she was almost fourteen, she had gone away from him.

'Col, don't kick the sand like that, it's flying everywhere. Why don't you go and have a swim? Why can't you find something to do? I do so dislike you just hovering over us like that.'

Jess had filled a small bucket with water from the rock pool, and now she bent down and began to pour it carefully into the moat. It splashed on to her bare feet and she wriggled her toes. Fay's baby bounced up and down with interest and pleasure in the stream of water and the crenellated golden castle.

Col kicked again more forcefully. The clods of sand hit the tower of the castle sideways, and, as it fell, crumbled the edges off the other towers and broke open the surrounding wall, so that everything toppled into the moat, clouding the water.

Jess got to her feet, scarlet in the face, ready to hit out at him.

'I hate you. *I hate you.*'

'Jess . . .'

'He wants to spoil everything, look at him, he doesn't want anyone else to enjoy themselves, he just wants to sulk and . . . I hate him.'

Col thought, I am filled with evil, there is no hope for me. For he felt himself completely taken over by the badness within him.

'*I hate you.*'

He turned away from his sister's wild face and her mouth which opened and shut over and over again to shout her rejection of him, turned away from them all and began to walk towards the caves at the far side of the cove. Above them were the cliffs.

Three-quarters of the way up there was a ledge around which the gannets and kittiwakes nested. He had never climbed up as high as this before. There were tussocks of grass, dried and bleached bone-pale by the sea winds, and he clung on to them and to the bumps of chalky rock. Flowers grew, pale wild scabious and cliff buttercups, and when he rested, he touched his face to them.

Above his head, the sky was enamel blue. The sea birds watched him with eyes like beads. As he climbed higher, the wash of the sea and the voices of those on the beach receded. When he reached the ledge, he got his breath and then sat down cautiously, legs dangling over the edge. There was just enough room for him. The surface of the cliff was hot on his back. He was not at all afraid.

His family were like insects down on the sand, little shapes of colour dotted about at random. Jess was a pink shape, the parasol was bottle-glass green, Fay and Fay's baby were yellow. For most of the time they were still, but once they all clustered around the parasol to look at something and then broke away again, so that it was like a dance. The other people on the beach were quite separate, each family kept itself to itself. Out beyond the curve of the cliff the beach lay like a ribbon bounded by the tide, which did not reach as far as the cove except in the storms of winter. They had never been here during the winter.

When Col opened his eyes again his head swam for a moment. Everything was the same. The sky was thin and clear. The sun shone. If he had gone to sleep he might have tipped over and fallen forwards. The thought did not frighten him.

But all was not the same, for now he saw his father had left the family group and was padding down towards the sea. The black hairs curled up the backs of his legs and the soles of his feet were brownish pink as they turned up one after the other.

Col said, do I like my father? And thought about it. And did not know.

Fay's baby was crawling after him, its lemon-coloured behind stuck up in the air.

Now, Col half-closed his eyes, so that air and sea and sand shimmered, merging together.

Now, he felt rested, no longer angry, he felt above it all.

Now, he opened his eyes again and saw his father striding into the water, until it reached up to his chest: then he flopped onto his belly and floated for a moment, before beginning to swim.

Col thought, perhaps I am ill and *that* is the badness within me.

But if he had changed, the others had changed too. Since Fay had married and had the baby and gone to live in Berkshire, she was different, she fussed more, was concerned with the details of things, she spoke to them all a trifle impatiently. And his mother was so languid. And Jess – Jess did not want his company.

Now he saw his father's dark head bobbing up and down quite a long way out to sea, but as he watched, sitting on the high cliff

ledge in the sun, the bobbing stopped – began again – an arm
came up and waved, though as if it were uncertain of its direction.

Col waved back.

The sun was burning the top of his head.

Fay and Fay's baby and Jess had moved in around the parasol
again, their heads were bent together. Col thought, we will never be
the same with one another, the ties of blood make no difference, we
are separate people now. And then he felt afraid of such truth.
Father's waving stopped abruptly, he bobbed and disappeared,
bobbed up again.

The sea was still as glass.

Col saw that his father was drowning.

In the end, a man from the other side of the beach went running
down to the water's edge and another to where the family were
grouped around the parasol. Col looked at the cliff, falling away at
his feet. He closed his eyes and turned around slowly and then got
down on his hands and knees and began to feel for a foothold,
though not daring to look. His head was hot and throbbing.

By the time he reached the bottom, they were bringing his father's
body. Col stood in the shadow of the cliff and shivered and smelled
the dank, cave smell behind him. His mother and Fay and Jess
stood in a line, very erect, like Royalty at the cenotaph, and in Fay's
arms the baby was still as a doll.

Everyone else kept away, though Col could see that they made
half-gestures, raised an arm or turned a head, occasionally took an
uncertain step forward, before retreating again.

Eventually he wondered if they had forgotten about him. The men
dripped water off their arms and shoulders as they walked and the
sea ran off the body, too, in a thin, steady stream.

Nobody spoke to him about the cliff climb. People only spoke of
baths and hot drinks and telephone messages, scarcely looking at
one another as they did so, and the house was full of strangers
moving from room to room.

In bed, he lay stiffly under the tight sheets and looked towards
the window where the moon shone. He thought, it is my fault. I
prayed for some terrible happening and the badness within me
made it come about. I am punished. For this was a change greater
than any he could have imagined.

When he slept he dreamed of drowning, and woke early, just at
dawn. Outside the window, a dove grey mist muffled everything. He
felt the cold linoleum under his feet and the dampness in his
nostrils. When he reached the bottom of the stairs he saw at once
that the door of the sun parlour was closed. He stood for a moment

outside, listening to the creaking of the house, imagining all of them in their beds, his mother lying alone. He was afraid. He turned the brass doorknob and went slowly in.

There were windows on three sides of the room, long and uncurtained, with a view of the sea, but now there was only the fog pressing up aganst the panes, the curious stillness. The floor was polished and partly covered with rush matting and in the ruts of this the sand of all the summer past had gathered and lay, soft and gritty, the room smelled of seaweed. On the walls, the sepia photographs of his great-grandfather the Captain, and his naval friends and their ships. He had always liked this room. When he was small, he had sat here with his mother on warm, August evenings, drinking his mug of milk, and the smell of stocks came in to them from the open windows. The deckchairs had always been in a row outside on the terrace, empty at the end of the day. He stepped forward.

They had put his father's body on the trestle, dressed in a shirt and covered with a sheet and a rug. His head was bare and lay on a cushion, and the hands, with the black hair over their backs, were folded together. Now, he was not afraid. His father's skin was oddly pale and shiny. He stared, trying to feel some sense of loss and sorrow. He had watched his father drown, though for a long time he had not believed it, the water had been so entirely calm. Later, he had heard them talking of a heart attack, and then he had understood better why this strong barrel of a man, down that day from the City, should have been so suddenly sinking, sinking.

The fog horn sounded outside. Then, he knew that the change had come, knew that the long, hot summer was at an end, and that his childhood had ended too, that they would never come to this house again. He knew, finally, the power of the badness within him and because of that, standing close to his father's body, he wept.

Family holidays

But the others were happy here. They slipped into the gentle, lazy routine of summer as their feet slipped into sandals, they never grew bored or angry or irritable, never quarrelled with one another.

Read

Read this poem and study the photographs which follow it.

The Beach

The agony and turmoil
of when family meet beach!
Argument of where to pitch
Of when to eat
Of what to play
Sand-infested lunches
Tar on every towel
Car boots full of festering sea shells
And claws of crabs and wood.
Parents sprawled where children pester
Hourly marches to the loos
Stones that cripple
Freezing water
Punctured air beds and broken flip-flops
High tide at mid-day
Itchy sandy walks back to the oven-like car
Bad tempered traffic-jams
Arguments as to which turning to go down
    No telly in the evening
    —boring game of cards.

SARAH WILSON, *CITY LINES*

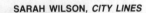

Talk

In groups talk about your own experiences of family holidays. How do they compare with the poem and photogaphs you have just studied?

How do you think the following characters in the story felt about their holiday before the death of Col's father:

● Jess
● Fay
● Col's mother?

What is the matter with Col?

Col thought, I hate it here. I hate it. I hate it. And he clenched his fist under cover of the table until the fingernails hurt him.

Talk

In pairs list as many possible reasons as you can for Col's unhappiness.

Read

Read the following extract by a teenager about the same age as Col's sister.

Maisy Hamilton

I'm a fourteen-year-old, one of many who never usually write to magazines or enter competitions, as to us it seems such a long shot at being printed or winning. None of my friends ever seem to win. At fourteen, I'm at the 'can't be bothered' stage where everything we set out to do is never done. When our mother says, 'lay the table', we can't even be bothered to reply; we're that lazy. I regard myself as a mature adult but to the old-fashioned parents I'm still *the kid*, which is the most aggravating name to call me. 'What would the child like to drink?' a waiter once asked my father. I wanted to turn round and say, 'Look here, matey boy, I'm an adult,' but being my usual timid self, I declined the opportunity. If I had, my mother would have turned round and said, 'Sorry, but she's at *that* age.' What is this 'that age'? My brother has been at 'that age' since he was ten and he now happens to be seventeen.

BITTERSWEET DREAMS

Talk

In groups talk about the feelings described by Maisy. Have you ever felt the same? If so tell the members of your group about those experiences.

Assignment

Imagine you are Col. Write a letter to a close friend in which you try to explain what it is that is making you unhappy.

Death by drowning

Father's waving stopped abruptly, he bobbed and disappeared, bobbed up again.

Talk

Col was shocked at the death of his father, a strong swimmer, but later finds out that a heart-attack caused him to drown. Col feels sure he is responsible for his father's death but does not know why. Talk about these possible explanations.

- Col feels that his own bad behaviour has driven his father to commit suicide.
- Col feels that God has answered his prayer and brought about an evil event.
- Col feels that if he had shouted, someone could have saved his father.
- Col feels that if he had not gone off on his own the family would have stayed together on the beach.
- Col feels that his own hostility to his father had driven him to swim alone.

Which do you think are most likely? Explain your choice. Are there any explanations that you can add?

What Colin fears

Col thought, we will never be the same with one another, the ties of blood make no difference, we are separate people now.

Read

Read this poem.

Not Waving But Drowning

Nobody heard him, the dead man,
But still he lay moaning;
I was much further out than you thought
And not waving but drowning

Poor chap he always loved larking
And now he's dead
It must have been too cold for him his heart gave way
They said

Oh, no no no, it was too cold always
(Still the dead one lay moaning)
I was much too far out all my life
and not waving but drowning.

STEVIE SMITH

Talk

This poem is about someone who dies under very similar circumstances to Col's father. Onlookers assume death was caused by heart failure but the poet imagines the dead man speaking and disagreeing with them. In pairs, decide what lines in the poem could be spoken by the dead man.

What line suggests that something was missing in the dead man's life? What do you think it was that was missing?

Write

Is the dead man in the poem more like Col or his father? List your reasons.

Assignment

Write a poem which explores your own relationship with a member of your family.

That certain age

Read

Find the following quotations in the story:

A This year, for the first time, Col felt the difference in age between them, he saw that Jess was changing, moving away from him to join the adults.

B How had he ever been able to bear it?

C Yet now, he wanted to do some violence in this house, he wanted an end to everything.

D When he was younger he had liked this room . . . but now it felt too small, it stifled him, it was a childish room, a pale, dead room in which nothing ever happened and nothing would change.

E He wants to spoil everything, look at him, he doesn't want anyone else to enjoy themselves, he just wants to sulk . . .

F Col thought, I'm filled with evil, there is no hope for me.

G But if he had changed, the others had changed too. Since Fay had married and had the baby and gone to live in Berkshire, she fussed more, was concerned with the details of things, she spoke to them all a trifle impatiently. And his mother was so languid. And Jess – Jess did not want his company.

H Then, he knew that the change had come, knew that the long, hot summer was at an end, and that his childhood had ended too . . .

Talk

In pairs make a list of all the ways in which you think:

● Col was changing;
● his family were changing.

Which of these quotations comes closest, in your view, to summing up the meaning of this story? Explain your reasons.

Assignment

Write a story about the end of childhood; your own or someone else's.

Cane Is Bitter

Samuel Selvon

In February they began to reap the cane in the undulating fields at Cross Crossing estate in the southern part of Trinidad. 'Crop time coming boy, plenty work for everybody,' men in the village told one another. They set about sharpening their cutlasses on grinding stones, ceasing only when they tested the blades with their thumb-nails and a faint ping! quivered in the air. Or they swung the cutlass at a drooping leaf and cleaved it. But the best test was when it could shave the hairs of your leg.

Everyone was happy in Cross Crossing as work loomed up in the way of their idleness, for after the planting of the cane there was hardly any work until the crop season. They laughed and talked more and the children were given more liberty than usual, so they ran about the barracks and played hide and seek in those canefields which had not yet been fired to make the reaping easier. In the evening, when the dry trash was burnt away from the stalks of sweet juice, they ran about clutching the black straw which rose on the wind: people miles away knew when crop season was on for the burnt trash was blown a great distance away. The children smeared one another on the face and laughed at the black streaks. It wouldn't matter now if their exertions made them hungry, there would be money to buy flour and rice when the men worked in the fields, cutting and carting the cane to the weighing-bridge.

In a muddy pond about two hundred yards east of the settlement, under the shade of spreading laginette trees, women washed clothes and men bathed mules and donkeys and hogcattle. The women beat the clothes with stones to get them clean, squatting by the banks, their skirts drawn tight against the back of their thighs, their saris retaining grace of arrangement on their shoulders even in that awkward position. Naked children splashed about in the pond, hitting the water with their hands and shouting when the water shot up in the air at different angles, and trying to make brief rainbows in the sunlight with the spray. Rays of the morning sun came slantways from halfway up in the sky, casting the shadow of trees on the pond, and playing on the brown bodies of the children.

Ramlal came to the pond and sat on the western bank, so that he squinted into the sunlight. He dipped his cutlass in the water and began to sharpen it on the end of a rock on which his wife Rookmin was beating clothes. He was a big man, and in earlier days was reckoned handsome. But work in the fields had not only tanned his

skin to a deep brown but actually changed his features. His nose
had a slight hump just above the nostrils, and the squint in his eyes
was there even in the night, as if he were peering all the time,
though his eyesight was remarkable. His teeth were stained brown
with tobacco, so brown that when he laughed it blended with the
colour of his face, and you only saw the lips stretched wide and
heard the rumble in his throat.

Rookmin was frail but strong as most East Indian women. She
was not beautiful, but it was difficult to take any one feature of her
face and say it was ugly. Though she was only thirty-six, hard work
and the bearing of five children had taken toll. Her eyes were black
and deceptive, and perhaps she might have been unfaithful to
Ramlal if the idea had ever occurred to her. But like most of the
Indians in the country districts, half her desires and emotions were
never given a chance to live, her life dedicated to wresting an
existence for herself and her family. But as if she knew the light she
threw from her eyes, she had a habit of shutting them whenever she
was emotional. Her breasts sagged from years of suckling. Her
hands were wrinkled and callous. The toes of her feet were spread
wide from walking without any footwear whatsoever: she never had
need for a pair of shoes because she never left the village.

She watched Ramlal out of the corner of her eye as he sharpened
the cutlass, sliding the blade to and fro on the rock. She knew he
had something on his mind, that was how he had come silently and
sat near to her pretending that he could add to the keenness of his
razor-sharp cutlass. She waited for him to speak, in an oriental
respectfulness. But from the attitude of both of them, it wasn't
possible to tell that they were about to converse, or even that they
were man and wife. Rookmin went on washing clothes, turning the
garments over and over as she pounded them on a flat stone, and
Ramlal squinted his eyes and looked at the sun.

At last, after five minutes or so, Ramlal spoke.

'Well, that boy Romesh coming home tomorrow. Is six months
since he last come home. This time, I make up my mind, he not
going back.'

Rookmin went on scrubbing, she did not even look up.

'You see how city life change the boy. When he was here the last
time, you see how he was talking about funny things?

Rookmin held up a tattered white shirt and looked at the sun
through it.

'But you think he will agree to what we are going to do?' she
asked. 'He must be learning all sorts of new things and this time
might be worse than last time. Suppose he want to take creole

wife?'

'But you mad or what? That could never happen. Ain't we make all arrangements with Sampath for Doolsie to married him? Anyway,' he went on, 'is all your damn fault in the first place, wanting to send him for education in the city. You see what it cause? The boy come like a stranger as soon as he start to learn all those funny things they teach you in school, talking about poetry and books and them funny things.'

'I did never want to send him for education, but it is you who make me do it.'

'Education is a good thing,' Rookmin said, without intonation. 'One day he might come lawyer or doctor, and all of we would live in a big house in the town, and have servants to look after we.'

'That is only foolish talk,' Ramlal said. 'You think he would remember we when he comes a big man? And besides, by that time you and me both dead. And besides, the wedding done plan and everything already.'

'Well, if he married Doolsie everything might work out.'

'How you mean if? I had enough of all this business. He have to do what I say, else I put him out and he never come here again. Doolsie father offering big dowry, and afterwards the both of them could settle on the estate and he could forget all that business.'

Rookmin was silent. Ramlal kept testing the blade with his nail, as if he were fascinated by the pinging sound, as if he were trying to pick out a tune.

But in fact he was thinking, thinking about the last time his son Romesh had come home . . .

It was only his brothers and sisters, all younger than himself, who looked at Romesh with wonder, wanting to ask him questions about the world outside canefields and the village. Their eyes expressed their thoughts, but out of some curious embarrassment they said nothing. In a way, this brother was a stranger, someone who lived far away in the city, only coming home once or twice a year to visit them. They were noticing a change, a distant look in his eyes. Silently, they drew aside from him, united in their lack of understanding. Though Romesh never spoke of the great things he was learning, or tried to show off his knowledge, the very way he bore himself now, the way he watched the cane moving in the wind was alien to their feelings. When they opened the books he had brought, eager to see the pictures, there were only pages and pages of words, and they couldn't read. They watched him in the night, crouching in the corner, the book on the floor near to the candle, reading. That alone made him different, set him apart. They thought he was going to be a pundit or a priest, or something extraordinary. Once his sister had asked: 'What do you read so much about, *bhai*?' and Romesh looked at her with a strange look and said, 'To tell you, you wouldn't understand. But have patience, a time will come soon, I hope, when all of you will learn to read and write.' Then Hari, his brother, said, 'Why do you feel we will not understand? What is wrong with our brains? Do you think because you go to school in the city that you are better than us? Because you get the best clothes to wear, and shoes to put on your feet, because you get favour from *bap* and *mai*?' Romesh said quickly, '*Bhai*, it is not that. It is only that I have left our village, and have learned about many things which you do not know about. The whole world goes ahead in all fields, in politics, in science, in art. Even now the governments in the West Indies are talking about federating the islands, and then what will happen to the Indians in this island? But we must not quarrel, soon all of us will have a chance.' But Hari was not impressed. He turned to his father and mother and said: 'See how he has changed. He don't want to play no games anymore, he don't want to work in the fields, he is too much of a bigshot to use a cutlass. His brothers and sisters are fools, he don't want to talk to them because they don't understand. He don't even want to eat we food again, this morning I see he ain't touch the *baghi*. No. We have to get chicken for him, and the cream from all the cows in the village. Yes, that is what. And who it is does sweat for him to get him pretty shirt to wear in Port of Spain?' He held up one of the girls' arms and spanned it with his fingers. 'Look how thin she is. All that is for you to be a big man, and now you scorning your own family?' Romesh got up from the floor and faced them. His eyes burned fiercely, and he looked like the pictures of Indian Gods the children had seen in the village hall. 'You are all wrong!' He cried in a ringing voice. 'Surely you, *bap*, and you, *mai*, the years must have taught you that you must make a different life for your children, that you must free them from ignorance and the wasting away of their lives? Do you want them to suffer as you have?' Rookmin looked like she was going to say something, but instead she shut her eyes tight. Ramlal said: 'Who tell you we suffer? We bring children in the world and we happy.' But Romesh went on, 'And what will the children do? Grow up in the village here, without learning to read and write? There are schools in San Fernando, surely you can send them there to learn about different things besides driving a mule and using a cutlass? Oh *bap*, we are such a backward people, all the others move forward to better lives, and we lag behind believing that what is to be, will be. All over Trinidad, in the country districts, our people toil on the land and reap the cane. For years it has been so, years in the same place, learning nothing new, accepting our fate like animals. Political men come from India and give speeches in the city. They speak of better things, they tell us to unite and strive for a greater goal. And what does it mean to you? Nothing. You are content to go hungry, to see your children run about naked, emaciated, grow up dull and stupid, slaves to your own indifference. You do not even pretend an interest in the Legislative Council. I remember why you voted for Pragsingh last year, it was because he gave you ten dollars – did I not see it for myself? It were better that we returned to India than stay in the West Indies and live such a low form of existence.' The family watched Romesh wide-eyed. Ramlal sucked his clay pipe noisily. Rookmin held her youngest daughter in her lap, picking her head for lice, and now and then shutting her eyes so the others wouldn't see what she was thinking. 'There is only one solution,' Romesh went on, 'We must educate the children, open up new worlds in their minds, stretch the horizon of their thoughts . . .' Suddenly he stopped. He realised that for some time now they weren't listening, his words didn't make any sense to them. Perhaps he was going about this in the wrong way, he would have to find some other way of explaining how he felt. And was he sufficiently equipped in himself to propose vast changes in the lives of the people? It seemed to him then how small he was, how there were so many things he didn't know. All the books he'd read, the knowledge he'd lapped up so hungrily in the city, listening to the politicians making speeches in the square – all these he mustered to his assistance. But it was as if his brain were too small, it was like putting your mouth in the sea and trying to drink all the water. Wearily, like an old man who had tried to prove his point merely by repeating, 'I am old, I should know,' Romesh sat down on the floor, and there was a silence in the hut, a great silence, as if the words he'd spoken had fled to the place and gone outside with the wind and the cane.

And so after he had gone back to the city his parents discussed the boy, and concluded that the only thing to save his senses was to marry him off. 'You know he like Sampath daughter from long time, and she is a hard-working girl, she go make good wife for him,' Rookmin had said. Ramlal had seen Sampath and everything was fixed. Everybody in the village knew of the impending wedding . . .

Romesh came home the next day. He had some magazines and books under his arm, and a suitcase in his hand. There was no reception for him; everyone who could work was out in the fields.

He was as tall as the canes on either side of the path on which he walked. He sniffed the smell of burning cane, but he wasn't overjoyful at coming home. He had prepared for this, prepared for the land on which he had toiled as a child, the thatched huts, the children running naked in the sun. He knew that these things were not easily forgotten which he had to forget. But he saw how waves of wind ripped over the seas of cane and he wondered vaguely about big things like happiness and love and poetry, and how they could fit into the poor, toiling lives the villagers led.

Romesh met his sisters at home. They greeted him shyly but he held them in his arms and cried, '*Beti*, do you not know your own brother?' And they laughed and hung their heads on his shoulder.

'Everybody gone to work,' one girl said, 'and we cooking food to carry. Pa and Ma was looking out since early this morning, they say to tell you if you can come in the fields.'

Romesh looked around the hut in which he had grown up. It seemed to him that if he had come home after ten years, there would still be the old table in the centre of the room, its feet sunken in the earthen floor, the black pots and pans hanging on nails near the window. Nothing would change. They would plant the cane, and when it grew and filled with sweet juice cut it down for the factory. The children would waste away their lives working with their parents. No schooling, no education, no widening of experience. It was the same thing the man had lectured about in the public library three nights before in the Port of Spain. The most they would learn would be to wield a cutlass expertly, or drive the mule cart to the railway line swiftly so that before the sun went down they would have worked sufficiently to earn more than their neighbours.

With a sigh like an aged man Romesh opened his suitcase and took out a pair of shorts and a polo shirt. He put them on and put the suitcase away in a corner. He wondered where would be a safe place to put his books. He opened the suitcase again and put them in.

It was as if, seeing the room in which he had argued and quarrelled with the family on his last visit, he lost any happiness he might have had on coming back this time. A feeling of depression overcame him.

It lasted as he talked with his sisters as they prepared food to take to the fields. Romesh listened how they stumbled with words, how they found it difficult to express themselves. He thought how regretful it was that they couldn't go to school. He widened the thought and embraced all the children in the village, growing up with such little care, running naked in the mud with a piece of *roti* in their hands, missing out on all the things that life should stand for.

But when the food was ready and they set off for the fields, with the sun in their eyes making them blind, he felt better. He would try to be happy with them, while he was here. No more preaching. No more voicing of opinion on this or that.

Other girls joined his sisters as they walked, all carrying food. When they saw Romesh they blushed and tittered, and he wondered what they were whispering about among themselves.

There were no effusive greetings. Sweating as they were, their clothes black with the soot of burnt canes, their bodies caught in the motions of their work, they just shouted out, and Romesh shouted back. Then Ramlal dropped the reins and jumped down from his cart. He curved his hand like a boomerang and swept it over his face. The soot from his sleeves smeared his face as he wiped away the sweat.

Rookmin came up and opened tired arms to Romesh. '*Beta*,' she cried as she felt his strong head on her breast. She would have liked to stay like that, drawing his strength and vitality into her weakened body, and closing her eyes so her emotion wouldn't show.

'*Beta*,' his father said, 'you getting big, you looking strong.' They sat down to eat on the grass. Romesh was the only one who appeared cool, the others were flushed, the veins standing out on their foreheads and arms.

Romesh asked if it was a good crop.

'Yes *Beta*,' Ramlal said. 'Is a good crop, and plenty of work for everybody. But this year harder than last year, because rain begin to fall early, and if we don't hurry up with the work, it will be too much trouble for all of us. The overseer come yesterday, and he say a big bonus for the man who do the most work. So everybody working hard for that bonus. Two of my mules sick, but I have to work them, I can't help. We trying to get the bonus.'

After eating Ramlal fished a cigarette out from his pocket and lit it carefully. First greetings over, he had nothing more to tell his son, for the time being anyway.

Romesh knew they were all remembering his last visit, and the things he had said then. This time he wasn't going to say anything, he was just going to have a holiday and enjoy it, and return to school in the city refreshed.

He said, 'Hari, I bet I could cut more canes than you.'

' Hari laughed. 'Even though I work the whole morning already is a good bet. You must forget to use *poya*, your hands so soft and white now.'

That is the way life is, Ramlal thought as Romesh took his cutlass. Education, school, *chut*! It was only work put in a *roti* in your belly, only work that brought money. The marriage would soon change Romesh. And he felt a pride in his heart as his son spat on the blade.

The young men went to a patch of burnt canes. The girls came too, standing by to pile the fallen stalks of sweet juice into heaps, so that they could be loaded quickly and easily on to the carts and raced to the weighing bridge.

Cane fell as if a machine were at work. The blades swung in the air, glistened for a moment in the sunlight, and descended on the stalks near the roots. Though the work had been started as a test of speed, neither of them moved ahead of the other. Sometimes Romesh paused until Hari came abreast, and sometimes Hari waited a few canes for Romesh. Once they looked at each other and laughed, the sweat on their faces getting into their mouths. There was no more enmity on Hari's part: seeing his brother like this, working, was like the old days when they worked side by side at all the chores which filled the day.

Everybody turned to in the field striving to outwork the others, for each wanted the bonus as desperately as his neighbour. Sometimes the women and the girls laughed or made jokes to one another, but the men worked silently. And the crane on the weighing bridge creaked and took load after load. The labourer manipulating it grumbled: there was no bonus for him, though his wage was more than that of the cane-cutters.

When the sun set all stopped work as if by signal. And in Ramlal's hut that night there was laughter and song. Everything was all right, they thought. Romesh was his natural self again, the way he swung that cutlass! His younger sisters and brother had never really held anything against him, and now that Hari seemed pleased, they dropped all embarrassment and made fun. See *bhai*, I make *meetai* especially for you,' his sister said, offering the sweetmeat.

'He work hard, he deserve it,' Hari agreed, and he looked at his brother, almost with admiration.

Afterwards, when Ramlal was smoking and Rookmin was searching in the youngest girl's head for lice ('put pitch-oil, that will kill them,' Ramlal advised), Romesh said he was going to pay Doolsie a visit.

There was a sudden silence. Rookmin shut her eyes, the children stopped playing, and Ramlal coughed over his pipe.

'Well what is the matter?' Romesh asked, looking at their faces.

'Well, now,' Ramlal began, and stopped to clear his throat. 'Well now, you know that is our custom, that a man shouldn't go to pay a visit to the girl he getting married . . .'

'What!' Romesh looked from face to face. The children shuffled their feet and began to get embarrassed at the stranger's presence once more.

Ramlal spoke angrily. 'Remember this is your father's house! Remember the smaller ones! Careful what you say, you must give respect! You not expect to get married one day, eh? Is a good match we make, boy, you will get good dowry, and you could live in village and forget them funny things you learning in the city.'

'So it has all been arranged,' Romesh said slowly. 'That is why everybody looked at me in such a strange way in the fields. My life already planned for me, my path pointed out – cane, labour, boy children, and the familiar village of Cross Crossing.' His voice had dropped lower, as if he had been speaking to himself, but it rose again as he addressed his mother: 'And you, *mai*, you have helped them to do this to me? You whose idea it was to give me an education?'

Rookmin shut her eyes and spoke. 'Is the way of our people, is we custom from long time. And you is Indian? The city fool your brains, but you will get back accustom after you married and have children.'

Ramlal got up from where he was squatting on the floor, and faced Romesh. 'You have to do what we say', he said loudly. 'Ever since you in the city, we notice how you change. You forgetting custom and how we Indian people does live. And too besides, money getting short. We want help on the estate. The garden want attention, and nobody here to see about cattle and them. And no work after crop, too besides.'

'Then I can go to school in San Fernando,' Romesh said desperately. 'If there is no money to pay the bus, I will walk. The government schools are free, you do not have to pay to learn.'

'You will be married and have boy children,' Ramlal said, 'and you will stop answering your *bap* . . .'

'*Hai*! *Hai*!' Drivers urged their carts in the morning sun, and whips cracked crisply on the air. Dew still clung to the grass as workers took to the fields to do as much as they could before the heat of the sun began to tell.

Romesh was still asleep when the others left. No one woke him; they moved about the hut in silence. No one spoke. The boys went to harness the mules, one of the girls to milk the cows and the other was busy in the kitchen.

When Romesh got up he opened his eyes in full awareness. He could have started the argument again as if no time had elapsed, the night had made no difference.

He went into the kitchen to wash his face. He gargled noisily scraped his tongue with his teeth. Then he remembered his toothbrush and toothpaste in his suitcase. As he cleaned his teeth his sister stood watching him. She never used a toothbrush: they broke a twig and chewed it to clean their mouths.

'You going away, *bhai*?' she asked him timidly.

He nodded, with froth in his mouth.

'If you stay, you could teach we what you know', the girl said.

Romesh washed his mouth and said, '*Baihin*, there are many things I have yet to learn.'

'But what will happen to us?'

'Don't ask me questions little sister,' he said crossly.

After he had eaten he left the hut and sulked about the village, walking slowly with his hands in his pockets. He wasn't quite sure what he was going to do. He kept telling himself that he would go away and never return, but bonds he had refused to think about surrounded him. The smell of burnt cane was strong on the wind. He went to the pond, where he and Hari used to bath the mules. What to do? His mind was in a turmoil.

Suddenly he turned and went home. He got his cutlass – it was sharp and clean, even though unused for such a long time. Ramlal never allowed any of his tools to get rusty.

He went out into the fields, swinging the cutlass in the air as if with each stroke he swept a problem away.

Hari said: 'Is time you come. Other people start work long time, we have to work extra to catch up with them.'

There was no friendliness in his voice now.

Romesh said nothing, but he hacked savagely at the canes, and in half an hour he was bathed in sweat and his skin scratched from contact with the cane.

Ramlal came up in the mule cart and called out, 'Work faster! We a whole cartload behind!' Then he saw Romesh and he came down from the cart and walked rapidly across. 'So you come! Is a good thing you make up your mind!'

Romesh wiped his face. 'I am not going to stay, *bap*.' It was funny how the decision came, he hadn't known himself what he was going to do. 'I will help with the crop, you shall get the bonus if I have to work alone in the night. But I am not going to get married. I am going away after the crop.'

'You are mad, you will do as I say.' Ramlal spoke loudly, and other workers in the field stopped to listen.

The decision was so clear in Romesh's mind that he did not say anything more. He swung the cutlass tirelessly at the cane and knew that when the crop was finished, it would be time to leave his family and the village. His mind got that far, and he didn't worry about after that . . .

As the wind whispered in the cane, it carried the news of Romesh's revolt against his parents' wishes, against tradition and custom.

Doolsie, working a short distance away, turned her brown face from the wind. But women and girls working near to her whispered among themselves and laughed. Then one of the bolder women, already married, said, 'Well girl, is a good thing in a way. Some of these men too bad. They does beat their wife too much – look at Dulcie husband, he does be drunk all the time, and she does catch hell with him.'

But Doolsie bundled the canes together and kept silent.

'She too young yet,' another said. 'Look, she breasts not even form yet!'

Doolsie did not have any memories to share with Romesh, and her mind was young enough to bend under any weight. But the way her friends were laughing made her angry, and in her mind she too had revolted against the marriage.

'All-you too stupid!' she said, lifting her head with a childish pride so that her sari fell on her shoulder. 'You wouldn't say Romesh is the only boy in the village! And too besides, I wasn't going to married him if he think he too great for me.'

The wind rustled through the cane. Overhead, the sun burned like a furnace.

bhai – brother
bap – dad
mai – mother
beta – son
roti – bread, chapati
baihin – big brother
meetai – a kind of sweet
poya – young sugar cane plant
beti – sister

Trinidad and sugar cane

Samuel Selvon said that one of the aims of this story was to expose the unhappy economic circumstances of families living on Trinidad in 1949. For many families it was necessary, not only for the adults but also for the children, to work on the sugar-cane estates.

Talk

Study the map of Trinidad to give you a clear idea of where the sugar-cane estates are located and where Port of Spain is. Talk about what impression of life on a sugar-cane estate you gain from the photograph which follows.

TRINIDAD

San Juan
Tunapuna
Port of Spain
Arima
Sangre Grande

Gulf
of
Paria

San Fernando
CROSS CROSSING
Brighton
Point
Fortin

Rio
Claro

Sugar cane
growing area

0   km   25

Women in Trinidad

Like most women of the Indians in the country districts, half her desires and emotions were never given a chance to live, her life dedicated to wresting an existence for herself and her family.

She waited for him to speak, in an oriental respectfulness.

Read

Read this description of how women in Trinidad were educated.

Before the abolition of slavery in the West Indies, education was essentially for the white and privileged classes. Popular education was only introduced in 1834. It was seen as necessary to provide the freed slaves with the knowledge of the social requirements for them to be absorbed into a free society.

The year 1851 marked the beginning of proper education for the island of Trinidad. Primary education was made generally available, and, between 1859 and 1870, a number of secondary schools – for boys only – were introduced. The only girls' school on the island was open solely to the daughters of wealthy landowners or important civil administrators. Only in 1911 was the girls' school opened to the public.

Education was directed at the needs of few, mainly male, wealthy Trinidadians. It followed the pattern of British schools, with women mainly being prepared for the role of housewife and companion.

Between 1916 and 1933 there was very little change in ideas in education for Trinidad. In 1933 a commission was set up to examine the education system of Trinidad. It concluded that, 'the present low status of women in the West Indies makes it the more important to secure essential equality of educational opportunity between the sexes'. For the first time it suggested that girls should not be denied lessons in Maths, Latin, Physics and Chemistry, so that they too could look for work in the professions.

JOYCELIN MASSIAN (ED), ADAPTED FROM *WOMEN AND EDUCATION*

Talk

In pairs describe your impression of what life was like for women on Trinidad in the 1940s after having read this article and *Cane Is Bitter*.

How typical of the women described by the commission do you think Rookmin was? Make a list of any similarities you find.

Make a list of everything Rookmin says in this story. What do these statements tell you about her opinions? Do you agree with them?

Role play

In pairs, imagine that you are Rookmin and one of her daughters. How would you be reacting to Romesh's return? Have the kind of conversation that you think they might have had while the men were not in the house.

Assignment

Write the story as you think it might have appeared to Rookmin. Explore her feelings and any frustrations she might have had with her role.

Difficult choices

Cane is Bitter was written in Trinidad in 1949, when I was still living on the island . . . it was one of my earliest attempts at 'conscious' writing – deliberately working on the story to incorporate social commentary, in this case . . . the caution with which East Indians approached education as it threatened their way of life.

SAMUEL SELVON

Write

In pairs, study these quotations from the story. Decide who said what. Makes notes on the different attitudes expressed in the story, using these headings:

● life in the town versus life in the country
● education
● change
● women

A 'He must be learning all sorts of new things . . .'

B 'I did never want to send him for education . . .'

C 'What do you read so much about, *bhai*?'

D To tell you, you wouldn't understand. But have a patience, a time will come soon, I hope, when all of you will learn to read and write.'

E 'We must educate the children, open up new worlds in their minds, stretch the horizons of their thoughts . . .'

F 'You know he like Sampath daughter from a long time, and she is a hard-working girl, she go make good wife for him . . .'

G 'You must forget to use the poya, your hands so soft and white

H 'Is the way of our people, is we custom from long time. And you is Indian? The city fool your brains, but you will get back accustom after you married and have children.'

I 'But what will happen to us?'

J 'You are mad, you will do as I say.'

K 'All-you too stupid!'

Talk

In groups talk about:

● what difficult choices face you in the next two years;
● what your parents' attitudes to education are and how they compare with your own (make a list of the areas where you disagree);
● who takes the decisions in your house.

What's in a title?

They would plant the cane, and when it grew and filled with sweet juice cut it down for the factory. The children would waste away their lives working with their parents. No schooling, no education, no widening of experience.

Read this poem by Faustin Charles.

Sugar Cane

The succulent flower bleeds molasses,
as its slender, sweet stalks bend,
beheaded in the breeze.

The green fields convulse golden sugar,
tossing the rain aside,
out-growing the sun,
and carving faces
in the sun-sliced panorama.

The reapers come at noon,
riding the cutlass-whip;
their saliva sweetens everything
in the boiling season.

Each stem is a flashing arrow,
swift in the harvest.

Cane is sweet sweat slain;
Cane is labour, unrecognised, lost and unrecovered;
sugar is the sweet swollen pain of the years;
sugar is slavery's immovable stain;
cane is water lying down
and water standing up.

Cane is a slaver;
cane is bitter,
very bitter, in the sweet blood of life.

ANDREW SALKEY (ED), *BREAKLIGHT*

Talk

In groups, make a list of all the things that the poem and the story have in common.

What do you think the poet thinks about sugar-cane? What does it mean for him?

How can cane taste bitter? Why do you think Samuel Selvon chose the title of this story? What do you think the messages of his story are?

Assignment

Write about what you think the story means. Use the discussions you have had, the information you have studied and anything else you can find out to help you. You could:

● write a poem;
● present your opinions in an essay;
● write a script of an imaginary interview with Romesh.

Arranged marriages

'So it has all been arranged,' Romesh said slowly. 'That is why everybody looked at me in such a strange way in the fields. My life already planned for me, my path pointed out . . .'

Read

In this story Romesh leaves home to continue his education. He decides to do this instead of entering into the marriage his parents have arranged with Doolsie. In these passages three British Asian women describe their views of arranged marriages. Read them carefully and then talk about the advantages and disadvantages of this system of choosing a partner.

If the Asian parent don't give enough freedom to the girl she is bound to do just what her parents don't want her to do, and I also think we should be able to marry the person we love not the person who our parents think is suitable. We should not have arranged marriages, after all this is not the old days, the past. But this is the present with the new generation not the old generation. You might think I am being silly to go out with this boy the third time but I am not being silly because I know what I am doing. He is the first boy I have fallen in love with. Why can't my parents just accept the fact that I love him and no one will stop me seeing him unless I die. Until then I won't stop seeing him. I have tried to talk about him but they won't listen, they think they know what is best for me. I have listened to what they had to say so now why can't they listen to what I've got to say, and the only other person I can talk to is my sister-in-law. She understands me and gives me good advice. Apart from her I don't think I could turn to anyone.

NARGIS

Marriage of course is a major topic of conversation for girls of my age, since hopefully, within the next few years we all hope to be married. My friends find my marriage arrangements interesting because they are never sure whether or not a marriage is to be arranged for me. My views on this subject have changed over the years. Until a few years ago I felt arranged marriages to be very unromantic and I couldn't understand how couples could be content with this arrangement. I then began speaking to girls who considered an arranged marriage to be acceptable, in some cases even desirable. Having increased in years and experience my views have been somewhat tempered. I now believe that, from reading recent statistics, 'love' marriages are not more successful than arranged marriages; however, I feel that it is the freedom of choice in a 'love' marriage that makes me covet one. I feel that I should have a complete choice in the man with whom I am to spend the rest of my life with, the chance to make up my own mind about the person I could be happy with, the freedom to decide my future be it right or the wrong choice.

RITA

When 'people' speak of arranged marriages, this is the example that they use as an area of culture conflict between the generations of an Asian society. I feel that conflict in this area is emphasised more than it exists. I have done a questionnaire project and found (amongst many other things) that more people are 'for' than 'against' marriages. What happens is that all bad news makes the media. The media and many others who study Asian youths speak as if they are bound to reject their culture if brought up in another country. But they forget that Asian individuals live within a family unit which is influential in the development of any individual. A person spends a lot of their life time with the family – especially if he/she is Indian.

I feel that being able to 'communicate' with my father has enabled me to adapt ideas suited to both an Indian and a British society – especially on ideas related to arranged marriages like most other Indian girls, when I was 16 years, I decided I wasn't going to have an arranged marriage. How could I marry someone I didn't know? Luckily for me, I have been able to have my questions answered through communication, and the exchange of ideas with older and equally aged persons to me. I feel that communication is essential if young people are to adopt the ideas of their elder generation. This is because there are no other people in the British society, that they can speak to, or that can understand the intricacies of the Indian culture. One thing that young people need to understand is that their parents were brought up in a society where arranged marriage was the only type they knew about. Thus, perhaps nobody spoke to them about arranged marriages; and this could make it difficult for them to speak on them. Therefore, young people should try to initiate a conversation.

I don't think parents should be blamed. Instead, they should be helped. I do not see myself as lucky to have understanding parents. It is all to do with forming a communicative relationship, actively on the part of me where some subjects are concerned. For a good relationship, there needs to be co-operation on both sides. People should remember that, like most other things, an arranged marriage is not all bad, nor all good. Arranged marriages are not primitive compared to love marriages. There are pros and cons for both. I have spoken of arranged marriages as I know – there is no single definition of an arranged marriage.

SHILA PATEL

Choosing a partner

Read

Arranged marriages affect women and men in many countries. Read these two letters from young Moroccans. What advice would you give them?

From *Beyond the Veil*

I am fifteen years old. A man came and asked for my hand from my parents. He has a bad temper and bad manners. He likes forbidden things like smoking, but kif. And of course my parents gave me to him. I have not accepted the marriage and I am not going to. But the problem is that when the contract is about to be written by the justice officer, they do not intend to let me know. They intend to take another girl and write a fake contract. Then I will be sacrificed. My last decision if they write the contract is definite. I will commit suicide to free myelf from these oppressive people. What does the religious law say concerning parents who fake their daughter's marriage? I prefer to kill myself whatever the law says.

* * *

I am employed as a clerk in a company. I have a father who lives in the country far from me. I met a girl I want to marry and I promised to marry her and she promised to marry me. I wrote to my father announcing the news, hoping that he would rejoice with me but he did not. He opposes the marriage. He wants me to marry a woman from the country. I cannot do that because I cannot conceive of my life without this girl anymore and if I try to part from her I might find myself in a situation which is dangerous not only for me but for the Muslim umma* as well, and for the Muslim religion too.

Please advise me about what is best for us and our religion.

*umma: community of believers

Seeking sanctuary

Read

Read this article from the *Guardian* (16.2.88).

Sanctuary girl allowed to stay

Tom Sharratt

A A GIRL of 13 from Bangladesh who took sanctuary in a Manchester church to avoid deportation has been given permission to stay permanently in Britain.

A Home Office spokesman said yesterday that a genetic fingerprint test had shown that Salema Begum of Oldham was in fact the daughter of the couple who claimed to be her parents.

Mr Timothy Renton, the minister of state responsible for immigration, had therefore decided to take the exceptional step of waiving the entry clearance requirement and allowing her to stay.

Salema's father, Mr Gura Miah, a cotton worker, was joined by his wife and five children in 1981. Salema stayed in Bangladesh with her grandmother but travelled to Britain in 1986 to join her family when her grandmother became to ill to look after her.

She took sanctuary in Choriton central church in Manchester last October and spent 10 days there before being granted an extension to her temporary permit to stay.

The Home Office spokesman said that her father had not originally declared her as one of his children and now admitted that one of the children who joined him in 1981 was not his son.

The campaign committee which has supported Salema said yesterday that her victory was being celebrated as an advance in the struggle for the rights of black people in Britain.

The committee will go ahead with a planned lobby of the Home Office today to draw attention to the plight of others threatened by deportation.

A spokeswoman said the campaign had been inspired by the action of Mr Viraj Mendis, aged 31, a Sri Lankan refugee who took sanctuary against deportation in another Manchester church 14 months ago.

Since then two other people besides Salema have taken sanctuary, in Bradford and Leicester.

Talk

In what ways is Salema Begum in a similar situation to that of Doolsie or Romesh in *Cane Is Bitter*?

Assignment

Imagine you are a reporter for the *Port of Spain Times*. Write an article about either Romesh or Doolsie for your paper.

● Imagine Doolsie or Romesh decides to seek some kind of sanctuary or escape from what their parents want to do.
● Use the situation described in the story as the starting-point for your ideas, but develop it in any way that you think it could have happened.
● Decide where your piece is set and who might have given advice.
● Explain how your newspaper became involved in the incident.

The Bottle Queen

W. P. Kinsella

When I was just a kid, my father, Paul Ermineskin, took off for the city, and I only seen him a few times in the last ten years. He hang around the bars and missions in the city and last time I seen him he was in bad shape and I didn't figure he had long left to live. So it sure is surprise when he come walking into the Hobbema Pool Hall one afternoon.

'Hey, Silas,' he say to me, and give my hand a shake. There is something sneaky about Pa, maybe it is the way he walks kind of sideways, with his eyes always darting all over the place. The weather is cold and it due to snow any minute but Pa is wearing only a red-silk western shirt, have black fringes all down the sleeves, and pants look like they come from a businessman's suit.

He buys a round of pop and Frito chips for me and my friends, tells us stories that make us laugh and shows us a new way to play 8-Ball that we never seen before. Pa smells of whisky, but he ain't drunk; in fact he looks healthier than I ever remember seeing him.

'You know I sure would like to see the other kids, Silas,' he say to me. 'I wonder if you might sort of ask your Ma if it would be okay?'

Pa smile at me when he say that and I can see that him and me look quite a lot alike. I frown some. Me and Ma and all the kids but Delores got more than our share of bad memories about Pa. Delores, she wasn't even born yet, though Ma's belly was big with her, when Pa left for good.

'Hey, Silas, look at me,' says Pa. 'You ever seen me lookin' so good? I straightened myself out some. Been off the booze and eatin' good meals. Even got a job lined up.' He smile again and slap me on the arm.

'A guy who's able to charm the warts off a toad,' is how Mad Etta, our medicine lady, describe Paul Ermineskin.

'Hmmfff,' Ma say when I tell her Pa is back on the reserve. 'He better not come around when he's drunk, if he know what's good for him.' Then when I mention he want to see the kids, 'They're all big enough to make their own minds up,' she says. 'Just let me know so's I can be away if he comes around.'

Of the kids, only Delores is interested. Thomas, and Hiram, and Minnie, young as they were, all have enough bad thoughts about Pa not to want to see him.

Pa stay with an old friend of his, Isaac Hide. He keep asking me for my sister Illianna's address in Calgary but I keep pretending I forgot to look it up. Illianna is married to a white man, live in a big, new house. Pa wouldn't be comfortable there.

Delores has never had a father, and I guess has always wished for one. She keep a picture of Jay Silverheels the movie actor, and Allen Sapp the artist, pinned to the wall, and I heard her tell a girlfriend once that the picture of Allen Sapp was really one of her father.

Pa and me was still a hundred yards from the cabin when Delores explode out the door and hang herself on his neck. If you want to see somebody get hugged, you look at Paul Ermineskin that afternoon. Delores glue herself to his hand and lead him around the reserve like he never been here before. She tell him all about how she is the best bottle collector there is, and show him the forty or so dozen beer bottles stacked by the side of the cabin.

Ordinarily, bottles left around like that would disappear real quick, but me and my friends Frank Fence-post and Rufus Firstrider let it be known anybody stealing from Delores have to deal with us. The younger kids is enough afraid, especially of Frank who like to act tough, that they leave things be.

People who know her, call Delores *The Bottle Queen*. That is because she is able to collect more beer bottles and pop bottles than anybody around the reserve.

'If you throw a bottle out the door of your cabin, Delores Ermineskin will catch it before it hits the ground,' Mad Etta say of her, and she say it with a prideful smile.

Delores take dancing lessons from Molly Thunder and Carson Longhorn. They is about the best chicken dancers around. Twice a week, Delores pack up her costume what Ma made out of an old dress, stuff it in a shopping bag comes from the Shoppers Drug Mart in Wetaskiwin, and head down to Blue Quills Hall for her lesson.

Carson Longhorn tell me she is really good. She win the prize for Girls Under 12 at our own pow-wow, and she win again, a five dollar prize, at the Rocky Mountain House rodeo. 'If she had the money to travel to more pow-wows, she'd win almost every time,' Carson tell me.

Delores is sometimes shy and sometimes bold. She can be as determined as a bird pulling a worm out of the ground. Her eyes is black and move fast as a crow's. She can spot a bottle in a ditch from a hundred yards. Sometimes when we drive back from Wetaskiwin or Ponoka, even at night, she spot a glint in the ditch, no more of a shine than a firefly, and she make me stop the truck. I watch her disappear into the ditch, walking real determined, hiking up her jeans, her pigtails what by that time of day coming undone, bouncing on her shoulders in the glow from the truck lights. In a minute she come back, usually with a bottle in each hand, grinning like somebody just give her a dollar. In winter, she can tell whether a hole in a snowdrift been made by wind, an animal, or a bottle. She wade right in, have almost to swim against the drifts sometimes, but she come out grip a bottle in her mitten, have snow on her clothes right up to the armpit.

Delores have a reason for collecting all the bottles she does. Molly Thunder, her dance teacher, also make costumes. Boy, at the pow-wows you see some dancers decked up in costumes make them look like a rainbow when they twirl around as they dance. Molly make those kind, fancy ones with real coloured feathers in the bustle and headdress, and the jackets and moccasins she makes be solid beadwork done on real buckskin. Molly sell them costumes for sometimes a thousand dollars and Indian dancers from all over Canada order their dancing dress from her.

Molly promise to sell Delores a costume at cost for only $300. 'A champion dancer should have fancy duds,' is what Molly says, and Delores she look at them costumes, finger the beadwork and feathers every time she at Molly's cabin.

'How can somebody who's only ten years old earn three hundred dollars?' Delores ask me. I suggest she collect bottles, but I thought she'd get tired of it in a few days, like kids do, not that she'd take her collecting serious as a religion. Every day after school she go off with her gunnysack dragging behind her and walk the ditches of Highway 2A either south or north from Hobbema. She also stay up late on weekend nights when people are partying and circulate from cabin to cabin. 'Soon as an empty or nearly empty bottle been set down on a table it disappears under Delores' coat,' people say. But they don't say it mean. Everybody is kind of proud to see a young girl work as hard as she does.

Sometimes Delores is like a growed up woman, especially when she is working, or counting her money which she collect in one dollar bills, ''Cause I look like I'm more rich that way.' Other times when she smile up at me showing how one of her big front teeth is only half-way grown in, she is like a little girl.

She is like a little girl with Pa. If being loved could make you a better person then Pa would be about equal to an angel. And Pa, I guess is affected some by the way she treat him. One day after him and Isaac Hide been to town drinking he give to Delores a barrette for her hair. It not an ordinary one, but is made from leather with pretty beads all over it. 'This here belong to your Grandma

Ermineskin,' I hear him tell Delores. 'She used to dance in all the pow-wows and was as good as anybody. Guess you take after her.'

Well, Delores couldn't of liked that barrette better if it was made of solid diamonds. She don't wear it in her hair but carry it on a thick string around her neck and show it to anybody she meet, whether they interested or not.

It make me mad to see Pa do that to her. It is the first I ever heard of my grandma being a dancer, though she did die before I was born and I don't know too much about her. But the idea of Pa carrying anything around with him for more than a month or so is not very likely. Pa, he don't own nothing but the clothes on his back, and when he's drunk I think he even sometimes lose some of them.

Him and Isaac Hide drink a lot at the Alice Hotel beer parlour the last couple of weeks and Pa look like he going back to his habit of not eating very often.

One afternoon when we hanging around the Hobbema Pool Hall, Bert Cardinal get off the southbound bus. Bert he been in jail for a few months for driving off with a car don't belong to him. 'Hey, Paul, what you up to since you got out?' is the first thing he say to my papa.

Pa try to pretend like he don't hear the question, but Bert carry right on in a loud voice. 'They had to throw Paul here out; he liked Fort Saskatchewan Jail so much he wanted to stay there permanent,' and he slap Pa on the back.

So now I know why he ain't been drinking for a year and been eating good. 'Hey, Silas,' Bert says, 'you should of seen your old man the day he got busted. Was walking out of Woodward's with a chainsaw in each hand. They give him eighteen months but they throw him out in twelve.'

I look at Pa. 'I never lied to you,' he says, 'you just never asked.' But he got a foxy look about him anyway.

Quite a few times I take Delores out in Louis Coyote's pickup truck, look for bottles. I stop on the shoulder of the road let Delores out, and she head off down the ditch in kind of a zig-zag run. I drive ahead exactly a mile, stop and walk the ditch ahead, putting bottles in the gunny-sack I'm dragging along. I'd only get a half-mile or so down the road when the truck catch up with me. I can see Delores kneeling on the front seat, grinning and steering as the truck bump down the shoulder. When she want to stop, she disappear from sight and I know she pressing with all her might on both the clutch and the brake.

One time I even complained to her about all the bottles she was collecting. 'You know me and Frank used to gather up bottles to buy gas for the truck,' I said. 'Now there ain't a bottle in all of Hobbema for us to find.' I was sorry right away that I said it, but me and Frank wanted to take our girls for a ride, and we was broke.

'You and Frank don't collect bottles, you steal them,' said Delores.

'Sometime Frank he borrow a case or two from somebody's yard . . .'

'Frank steals,' said Delores, sounding like a nun or a school teacher.

After supper that night Delores come into our cabin with four cases of beer bottles stacked in her arms like cord-wood. I couldn't even see her face behind them.

'I'm sorry, Silas,' she said. 'These will give you enough gas money to get to town and back,' and she set the bottles on the table and lean in and kiss my cheek. Of course I didn't take them, even though I really would of liked to.

One afternoon in the pool hall Pa he is bragging about how him and Isaac Hide going into business together, when I hit him up about giving that barrette to Delores. I checked with Ma and Mad Etta and they say Grandma Ermineskin, though she could build a teepee and run a cross-cut saw like a man, was never one to dance. 'Why'd you tell Delores that?' I ask. 'You know she gonna find you out for a liar.' I notice Pa is still wearing that red shirt with the fringes; the silky material got a fine glaze of dirt over it now. 'Hey, who's gonna tell her?' say Pa, 'you?'

'It don't be long until Delores recognize that barrette as something come from a craft-store in Wetaskiwin,' I say.

'She's just a little girl,' says Pa. 'Leave her be.' And he look mean at me out of his bloodshot eyes.

Next afternoon Delores talk me into driving her and her bottles into Wetaskiwin to the bottle depot. An old man in a dirty parka and a long-billed red cap tote up her take, which come to $49 and she take it all in ones as usual.

'Only thirty more dollars and I got enough for my costume,' she announce as we driving back. I try to talk her into spend a dollar or two for some burgers and Cokes but she won't do it.

We return Louis Coyote's truck to him and walk back to our cabin. Soon as we walk into the cabin I know something is wrong. There is a rustling noise from Delores' and Minnie's room, which is marked off by a sheet been throwed over some clothes-line cord.

When I move aside the sheet there is Paul Ermineskin, on his hands and knees, busy stuffing money into his pockets. Delores she keep her costume money stashed safe in a Kellogg's Corn Flake box, under some clothes on the floor of her room.

'What are you doing?' I yell, though there is no need to ask.

Pa look up and make kind of sick smile. 'Hey, I was just counting the money for the kid, ya know.'

If I looked at him any meaner he'd be deep-fried.

'I thought you was low-down the last time I seen you,' I say.

'Hey, I was gonna pay her back . . .'

Delores has followed me across the cabin and now she hangs on to my arm, real tight, and sniffles some. She looks at Pa, her eyes wide, not understanding. 'All you had to do was ask,' she say in a small, tear-choked voice.

'I was doing it for you,' Pa says to Delores. 'This other guy and me we going to go out and cut Christmas trees. We got a chance to make a lot of money . . .' and his voice kind of trail off. The money is laying there all mixed in with Delores' clothes. Pa takes some dollars from his shirt pocket and throws them down.

'Well, I better get going,' Pa says, standing up, 'got to head for Edmonton, find my partner and get to work.' He push past me and head for the door.

'No,' says Delores, 'don't go yet.' She let go of my arm, run over scoop up some money and hold it out to Pa, who has stopped and turned around.

Pa flash a smile at her, like a weasel just been invited into a hen house.

'You don't want to give him nothing, Delores,' I say.

'Yes, I do,' she say, real final like.

'You know, I'm gonna pay you back,' says Pa, smiling again.

I got my fists clenched, and even though I hardly ever raise up my hand against anybody, right now I'd like to punch that smile right through to the back of his neck.

'Just go,' says Delores, pushing more money at Pa who is stuffing it in all his pockets, even pushing some down the neck of his shirt what don't have no buttons on the front. When Pa got the money all stashed he wheel around and skulk out the door, giving us a little wave over his shoulder.

When he can't hear his boots on the snow no more, Delores rush over and throw her arms around me and hug real hard. She sob loud into my chest.

Maybe she have just the slightest suspicion he was telling the truth. After a while her crying slow down some. I tip her head up so I can see her face, and kiss her forehead. She looks so much like Pa. Maybe that was it, maybe she can feel his blood travelling around in her.

She is wearing that beaded barrette Pa gave her, not in her hair, but hanging from around her neck, it rest in a spot where she gonna grow breasts in a couple of years.

Still sniffling, she undo the barrette and hold it in the palm of her hand.

'Did this really belong to my Grandma Ermineskin, Silas?' she say to me, looking me right in the face with her wet, black eyes.

This is sure my chance to tan Paul Ermineskin's hide. And I'm mad enough to do it. But when I look at Delores it seem to me she lost enough already today. I can't believe she doesn't know the truth. I think the woman in her does, but it is the little girl who is asking the question. And if she has to ask I know what answer she want to hear.

8-ball – a kind of pool or billiards
pow-wow – social gatherings
rodeo – a round-up of cattle, when cow-handling skills are displayed
teepee – Indian tent made of stretched skins
barrette – bar-shaped hair-clip

Canada's Indians

The Indians were the original inhabitants of Canada.

Read

Read this account of their history and study the map, pictures and newspaper extracts which follow it.

The Europeans' contribution to the Indians

With the coming of Europeans to the New World, the way of life of the Indians began to change and in time changed radically. The earliest alterations were brought about by trade goods, especially metal tools. These diffused rapidly from group to group, often before the Indians had met Europeans. And to obtain them, the Indian exchanged furs which caused other changes in his way of life. In some ways, the introduction of trade goods was beneficial in that it made the Indians' work easier. But at the same time contact with Europeans was disastrous. A variety of diseases, especially smallpox against which the Indians had little or no resistance, soon began to sweep through the country, killing all ages by the thousands. Only recently has disease been successfully checked.

Another disturbing factor was the railroads. These forced the Indians to move from their lands. Railroads also made possible the more effective colonization of the southern part of Canada by farmers, who soon took over much of the lands held by the Indians. Furthermore, wildlife was needlessly slaughtered, such as the bison and passenger pigeon. This produced great hardship for the Indians and often brought starvation.

With these developments, the Indian was no longer able to be self-sufficient. Accordingly, the government entered into Treaties with the Indians by which they were assigned to Reserves. No longer were they free to travel their former lands securing their own livelihood. When this occurred, the Indians' way of life became disrupted and disorganized and the Indian dispirited. The low point in terms of numbers and general living conditions occurred about the turn of the present century. But with renewed interest on the part of the governments, both federal and provincial, the Indian has been cared for to a greater extent than ever before. He has been given greater educational opportunities, health measures have been introduced and housing and other government programs started in an attempt to better his lot. Although much is being done, more has to be done, especially in the education of Euro-Canadians, before the Indian can take his rightful place in Canadian society.

The Indian today

At present, there are approximately 250,000 Treaty Indians and an estimated 200,000 non-Treaty individuals of Indian ancestry. The population today probably nearly equals what is was at the time of European contact.

Many of the Indians, both Treaty and non-Treaty, live on reserves assigned to them by the government. But more and more are moving away from the reserves either into nearby communities or to large urban centres where they are attempting to make a life for themselves. Some are attaining an advanced education so as to become lawyers, doctors, teachers, nurses, politicians, geologists, farmers and construction workers in high steel. Some have succeeded but a large proportion of them remain in the lower economic strata and often find it necessary to depend upon welfare, a condition they do not wish to endure. They no longer retain, nor can they, their old way of life, but they have, however, retained many of the basic values that their ancestors held. They now wish to establish an ethnic identity of their own and take their place in a multi-cultural society – Canada.

EDWARD S. ROGERS, *THE INDIANS OF CANADA: A SURVEY*

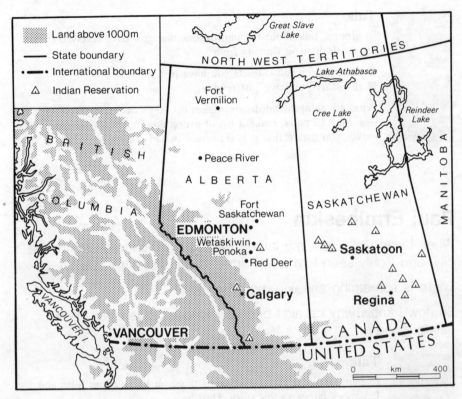

Indian reserves in Alberta and Saskatchewan

Indians Increasing, Attention Required

One of Canada's most successful Indians last night said that the state of Indian reserves had fallen so low that "you couldn't raise a disturbance on one if you irrigated it with whisky".

Dr G C Monture, a blood Mohawk and one of Canada's foremost leaders was addressing the Port Arthur Canadian Club at Prince Arthur.

"The Indian cannot understand the white man's greed and avarice. The Indian depended on mobility. He cannot understand why some women have 10 or 15 dresses and still have nothing to wear," said Dr Monture.

"The Indian never has had a pride of possession for the simple sake of possession. It was never what you think you need but what you know you need".

Dr Couture said that the Indian had been mistreated and exemplified the fact by stating that Manhattan Island was bought from the Indian for some beads and two bottles of rum.

And speaking of liquor he said that the introduction of "fire-water" and rifles added much to the decline of the Indian race.

Shameful Utter Disgrace

The plight of the Northwest Ontario Indians is general among Indians elsewhere, as repeated surveys and statistics show. In Canada as a whole, only one Indian home in eight has running water, fewer than half have electricity and 16% of Indian families live in one room shacks. Poverty breeds poverty, lack of training and education for jobs perpetuates apathy and public neglect or disregard compounds the misery.

Our land is everything to us. It is the only place where Cheyennes remember the same things together.

CHEYENNE LEADER

Talk

In groups, talk about the impressions that you have received of life for the Indians in Canada from:

● the pictures and extracts you have just studied;
● the story you have just read.

What advantages and disadvantages do they have, compared with your own life? In pairs, make a list of everything in *The Bottle Queen* that makes you aware that it is set on an Indian reserve.

Paul Ermineskin

When I was just a kid, my father, Paul Ermineskin, took off for the city, and I only seen him a few times in the last ten years.

There is something sneaky about Pa . . .

So now I know why he ain't been drinking for a year and been eating good . . .

Talk

In pairs, make a list of everything that you know about Silas and Dolores's father in this story. Desribe:

(a) his attitudes towards his wife and children;
(b) the different attitudes of Ma, Thomas, Hiram, Minnie, Silas and Dolores to him.

What kind of a father do you think Paul Ermineskin was?

Read

Read this explanation of the behaviour of some Indian fathers.

Sometimes a native father deserts his family in despair because his role and rights as a man and as a breadwinner have been completely eroded. Because of the colonial system, worthwhile employment is denied him, and he is prevented from being restored to his status in the family. He turns to desertion or alcohol to escape from his failures. Giving way to their feelings like this can often get natives into more trouble than they were in before; as a result they become distrustful of emotional experiences, develop 'stoical' attitudes, and caution themselves in their responses, emotions, and personal relationships. This, in turn, makes it difficult for them to relate honestly to other people, including members of their own family.

HOWARD ADAMS, *PRISON OF GRASS*

Does this alter your view of Paul Ermineskin as a father?

Assignment

It would be easy to obtain a very incomplete view of the Native Indians of Canada from the limited information presented here. Using your school and local library and any other source you can think of research some information about Canada's Indians. Present your research in the form of:

● *either* an article for a teenage magazine about teenage Indian life;
● *or* a radio documentary about Canadian Indians, aiming to inform people of your own age.

The two sides of Delores

Delores has never had a father, and I guess has always wished for one.

Delores is sometimes shy and sometimes bold.
Sometimes Delores is like a growed up woman. . .
She is like a girl with Pa . . .

Role play

The Bottle Queen is told through the eyes of Silas Ermineskin. In pairs, imagine that Silas and a friend are discussing Delores. Pa has just arrived on the reserve after an absence of three years and Silas is worried about the side of his sister's character which seems to surface on his surprise returns. Talk about what it is in Delores that shows how determined she is and what seems to happen to her when Pa is around. Imagine that one of you is Silas, one is his friend and have the conversation that they might have had.

Talk

Why do you think the story is called *The Bottle Queen*?

In groups, talk about the determination shown by Delores in her bottle-collecting. Why does she do it? How likely is she to achieve her aim? What evidence is there for this in the story? Describe any friend of yours whom you would consider to be determined. What qualities do they share with those you can see demonstrated by Delores?

Indian writing

Read

Read these two pieces of writing by Indian women.

Billie

Amid the chipped paint, and
dull smells of the tenement,
Billie sits contemplating
the blue sky
that barely shows.
A long time ago, Billie
sat on an old wooden chair
beside an oilcloth covered table
and smelled fresh bannock.
Billie slept on a ragged
mattress with three brothers
and one sister.
In the night, when the winter wind
blew, they huddled under
faded quilts to keep warm.
When they went to town,
they saw warm houses,
saw bread in bags,
saw cars that didn't rattle.

Billie wanted more, so . . .
at sixteen Billie went to work
in the city and got
a cheap room to save money
for the good things and,
the folks back home.

Billie sits and looks at
the cement below,
the cracked windows,
the decrepit garbage cans,
and hears the bark of a dog
above the incessant sounds
of the traffic.

Back home, the silence was
broken by the sounds of
laughing children and
barking dogs.
You could run over the hills,
see the sky,
smell the fresh wind
but . . .

A tear falls from sad brown eyes
that remember the five years,
of cheap rooms, lurid smells
of petty jobs and nasty men
but still she stays, trying
to make dreams realities.
'Someday I'll drive home
in a big car and
expensive clothes.
I'll make it someday.'

Billie wipes her eyes
and all that remains
of her memories
is the blue sky
that barely shows . . .

SEALEY/KIRKREES (EDS) *INDIANS WITHOUT TIPIS*

My mother died in 1948 at the age of 52. When I visited her in the hospital in Prince Albert, I knew it was the last time I would see her alive. In the previous couple of years I had discarded my parents; I had even given up visiting them. They reminded me of everything that was halfbreed. I was making it in the white world and I didn't want anything holding me down. All my friends were white, especially girl friends. I had a car and an apartment in the city; I had shaken off the ugliness of Indianness. I couldn't afford the albatross of a halfbreed heritage. One bad move could destroy years of cautious progress into mainstream society. My mother was completely halfbreed. All you had to do was look at her – her appearance, her manners, her clothes, her speech – everything gave her away as a halfbreed, yet she was still the most precious person in the world to me. She had given me the power to love and an appreciation of love in the most profound and sensitive way, and I had cast her aside, denied her existence. Now she was lying on her deathbed in great agony. Those 52 years of hunger and anguish and sacrifice were taking their toll.

Once outside the hospital, I broke into crying, violent crying. I cried so long that I thought I would vomit. Now I hated myself for what I had done – discarding my mother so that I could pretend to be white, free, and happy in mainstream society. I realized for the first time what the white-supremacist system had done to me, how it had perverted my sense of values and twisted the most beautiful relationship between two people. I puzzled over the tragic scene until my head was about to explode. I was tortured. I couldn't explain it to my mother: I thought she wouldn't understand. But perhaps she had understood all the time and had suffered in silence. Perhaps she understood how halfbreed mothers are swept aside for the froth and frills of white mainstream society. But she asked no questions about my absence. She didn't ask me if I had finally returned as her halfbreed son or if I was home to stay or if I was home in spirit as well. She didn't ask me to repent or apologize for rejecting her halfbreed home. She was just overjoyed to see her son – she was the mother I had always known, full of love and forgiveness, who had devoted her life to her family.

Standing in front of that hospital, I suddenly realized the fakery of my 'white' life and why I had developed a contempt for my Indianness. It took my mother's death to make me realize what my mockery and ridicule of halfbreed life had done to me. My entire body was in a rage. Somebody had to suffer for this. If I had had a machine gun, I would have raced through the streets of Prince Albert spraying bullets. But were the people on the street to blame? Had they made my mother suffer? Had they tortured her to death? If not, then who was to blame? Does it matter when there is such rage and hostility? To vent that rage is the only important thing and no one thinks about the consequences. Why did my mother have to die at the age of 52? Even so, she had already lived nearly 20 years beyond the life expectancy of most native people.

I remembered the sufferings and violence my mother had experienced. She had shed many tears because her children had to go to bed hungry. I had often seen her cut a small bannock loaf into six equal parts – one for each member of the family, including herself. But she would not eat her piece. Instead, she kept it until all the others had been eaten; then she would further divide her small slice into four parts, one for each of the children, and hand them out. Tears flowed from her eyes during this act of sacrifice and I never knew if they were tears of hunger or pity or shame or the fear of starvation the following day.

HOWARD ADAMS, *PRISON OF GRASS*

Assignment

Using either of these two pieces written by native Indians to give you ideas, produce a piece of writing about Delores. You could:
● write a poem about Delores as she sits crying over what happened; or
● write an account from Delores's point of view, set some years in the future, in which she reflects on what her father or mother meant to her now that they are dead.

Talk

And if she has to ask I know what answer she wants to hear.

How do you think Silas answers Delores's question about her barrette at the end of the story? What do you think happened next?

Assignment

Using what you have learned about Canadian Indians, continue *The Bottle Queen*. Produce a second short story of your own in which you develop some or all of the characters you have met in W. P. Kinsella's story.

Games at Twilight

Anita Desai

It was still too hot to play outdoors. They had had their tea, they
had been washed and had their hair brushed, and after the long
day of confinement in the house that was not cool but at least a
protection from the sun, the children strained to get out. Their faces
were red and bloated with the effort, but their mother would not
open the door, everything was still curtained and shuttered in a way
that stifled the children, made them feel that their lungs were stuffed
with cotton wool and their noses with dust and if they didn't burst
out into the light and see the sun and feel the air, they would
choke.

'Please, ma, please,' they begged. 'We'll play in the veranda and
porch – we won't go a step out of the porch.'

'You will, I know you will, and then—'

'No – we won't, we won't,' they wailed so horrendously that she
actually let down the bolt of the front door so that they burst like
seeds from a crackling, over-ripe pod into the veranda, with such
wild, maniacal yells that she retreated to her bath and the shower of
talcum powder and the fresh sari that were to help her face the
summer evening.

They faced the afternoon. It was too hot. Too bright. The white walls
of the veranda glared stridently in the sun. The bougainvillea hung
about it, purple and magenta, in livid balloons. The garden outside
was like a tray made of beaten brass, flattened out on the red
gravel and the stony soil in all shades of metal – aluminium, tin,
copper and brass. No life stirred at this arid time of day – the birds
still drooped, like dead fruit, in the papery tents of the trees; some
squirrels lay limp on the wet earth under the garden tap. The
outdoor dog lay stretched as if dead on the veranda mat, his paws
and ears and tail all reaching out like dying travellers in search of
water. He rolled his eyes at the children – two white marbles rolling
in the purple sockets, begging for sympathy – and attempted to lift
his tail in a wag but could not. It only twitched and lay still.

Then, perhaps roused by the shrieks of the children, a band of
parrots suddenly fell out of the eucalyptus tree, tumbled frantically in
the still, sizzling air, then sorted themselves out into battle formation
and streaked away across the white sky.

The children, too, felt released. They too began tumbling, shoving,
pushing against each other, frantic to start. Start what? Start their

business. The business of the children's day which is – play.

'Let's play hide-and-seek.'

'Who'll be It?'

'You be It.'

'Why should I? You be—'

'You're the eldest—'

'That doesn't mean—'

The shoves became harder. Some kicked out. The motherly Mira intervened. She pulled the boys roughly apart. There was a tearing sound of cloth but it was lost in the heavy panting and angry grumbling and no one paid attention to the small sleeve hanging loosely off a shoulder.

'Make a circle, make a circle!' she shouted, firmly pulling and pushing till a kind of vague circle was formed. 'Now clap!' she roared and, clapping, they all chanted in melancholy unison: 'Dip, dip, dip – my blue ship—' and every now and then one or the other saw he was safe by the way his hands fell at the crucial moment – palm on palm, or back of hand on palm – and dropped out of the circle with a yell and a jump of relief and jubilation.

Raghu was It. He started to protest, to cry 'You cheated – Mira cheated – Anu cheated—' but it was too late, the others had all already streaked away. There was no one to hear when he called out, 'Only in the veranda – the porch – Ma said – Ma *said* to stay in the porch!' No one had stopped to listen, all he saw were their brown legs flashing through the dusty shrubs, scrambling up brick walls, leaping over compost heaps and hedges, and then the porch stood empty in the purple shade of the bougainvillea and the garden as empty as before; even the limp squirrels had whisked away, leaving everything gleaming, brassy and bare.

Only small Manu suddenly reappeared, as if he had dropped out of an invisible cloud or from a bird's claws, and stood for a moment in the centre of the yellow lawn, chewing his finger and near to tears as he heard Raghu shouting, with his head pressed against the veranda wall, 'Eighty-three, eighty-five, eighty-nine, ninety . . .' and then made off in a panic, half of him wanting to fly north, the other half counselling south. Raghu turned just in time to see the flash of his white shorts and the uncertain skittering of his red sandals, and charged after him with such a blood-curdling yell that Manu stumbled over the hosepipe, fell into its rubber coils and lay there weeping, 'I won't be It – you have to find them all – all – All!'

'I know I have to, idiot,' Raghu said, superciliously kicking him with his toe. 'You're dead,' he said with satisfaction, licking the beads of perspiration off his upper lip, and then stalked off in

search of worthier prey, whistling spiritedly so that the hiders should
hear and tremble.

Ravi heard the whistling and picked his nose in a panic, trying to
find comfort by burrowing the finger deep-deep into that soft tunnel.
He felt himself too exposed, sitting on an upturned flower pot
behind the garage. Where could he burrow? He could run around
the garage if he heard Raghu come – around and around and
around – but he hadn't much faith in his short legs when matched
against Raghu's long, hefty, hairy footballer legs. Ravi had a
frightening glimpse of them as Raghu combed the hedge of crotons
and hibiscus, trampling delicate ferns underfoot as he did so. Ravi
looked about him desperately, swallowing a small ball of snot in his
fear.

The garage was locked with a great heavy lock to which the
driver had the key in his room, hanging from a nail on the wall
under his work-shirt. Ravi had peeped in and seen him still
sprawling on his string-cot in his vest and striped underpants, the
hair on his chest and the hair in his nose shaking with the vibrations
of his phlegm-obstructed snores. Ravi had wished he were tall
enough, big enough to reach the key on the nail, but it was
impossible, beyond his reach for years to come. He had sidled
away and sat dejectedly on the flower pot. That at least was cut to
his own size.

But next to the garage was another shed with a big green door.
Also locked. No one even knew who had the key to the lock. That
shed wasn't opened more than once a year when Ma turned out all
the broken bits of furniture and rolls of matting and leaking buckets,
and the white ant hills were broken and swept away and Flit
sprayed into the spider webs and rat holes so that the whole
operation looked like the looting of a poor, ruined and conquered
city. The green leaves of the door sagged. They were nearly off
their rusty hinges. The hinges were large and made a small gap
between the door and the walls – only just large enough for rats,
dogs and, possibly, Ravi to slip through.

Ravi had never cared to enter such a dark and depressing
mortuary of defunct household goods seething with such
unspeakable and alarming animal life but, as Raghu's whistling
grew angrier and sharper and his crashing and storming in the
hedge wilder, Ravi suddenly slipped off the flower pot and through
the crack and was gone. He chuckled aloud with astonishment at
his own temerity so that Raghu came out of the hedge, stood silent
with his hands on his hips, listening, and finally shouted 'I heard

you! I'm coming! *Got* you—' and came charging round the garage only to find the upturned flower pot, the yellow dust, the crawling of white ants in a mud-hill against the closed shed door – nothing. Snarling, he bent to pick up a stick and went off, whacking it against the garage and shed walls as if to beat out his prey.

Ravi shook, then shivered with delight, with self-congratulation. Also with fear. It was dark, spooky in the shed. It had a muffled smell, as of graves. Ravi had once got locked into the linen cupboard and sat there weeping for half an hour before he was rescued. But at least that had been a familiar place, and even smelt pleasantly of starch, laundry and, reassuringly, of his mother. But the shed smelt of rats, ant hills, dust and spider webs. Also of less definable, less recognizable horrors. And it was dark. Except for the white-hot cracks along the door, there was no light. The roof was very low. Although Ravi was small, he felt as if he could reach up and touch it with his finger tips. But he didn't stretch. He hunched himself into a ball so as not to bump into anything, touch or feel anything. What might there not be to touch him and feel him as he stood there, trying to see in the dark? Something cold, or slimy – like a snake. Snakes! He leapt up as Raghu whacked the wall with his stick – then, quickly realizing what it was, felt almost relieved to hear Raghu, hear his stick. It made him feel protected.

But Raghu soon moved away. There wasn't a sound once his footsteps had gone round the garage and disappeared. Ravi stood frozen inside the shed. Then he shivered all over. Something had tickled the back of his neck. It took him a while to pick up the courage to lift his hand and explore. It was an insect – perhaps a spider – exploring *him*. He squashed it and wondered how many more creatures were watching him, waiting to reach out and touch him, the stranger.

There was nothing now. After standing in that position – his hand still on his neck, feeling the wet splodge of the squashed spider gradually dry – for minutes, hours, his legs began to tremble with the effort, the inaction. By now he could see enough in the dark to make out the large solid shapes of old wardrobes, broken buckets and bedsteads piled on top of each other around him. He recognized an old bathtub – patches of enamel glimmered at him and at last he lowered himself onto its edge.

He contemplated slipping out of the shed and into the fray. He wondered if it would not be better to be captured by Raghu and be returned to the milling crowd as long as he could be in the sun, the light, the free spaces of the garden and the familiarity of his brothers, sisters and cousins. It would be evening soon. Their games would become legitimate. The parents would sit out on the lawn on cane basket chairs and watch them as they tore around the garden or gathered in knots to share a loot of mulberries or black, teeth-splitting *jamun* from the garden trees. The gardener would fix the hosepipe to the water tap and water would fall lavishly through the air to the ground, soaking the dry yellow grass and the red gravel and arousing the sweet, the intoxicating scent of water on dry earth – that loveliest scent in the world. Ravi sniffed for a whiff of it. He half-rose from the bathtub, then heard the despairing scream of one of the girls as Raghu bore down upon her. There was the sound of a crash, and of rolling about in the bushes, the shrubs, then screams and accusing sobs of, 'I touched the den—' 'You did not—' 'I did—' 'You liar, you did *not*' and then a fading away and silence again.

Ravi sat back on the harsh edge of the tub, deciding to hold out a bit longer. What fun if they were all found and caught – he alone left unconquered! He had never known that sensation. Nothing more wonderful had ever happened to him than being taken out by an uncle and bought a whole slab of chocolate all to himself, or being flung into the soda-man's pony cart and driven up to the gate by the friendly driver with the red beard and pointed ears. To defeat Raghu – that hirsute, hoarse-voiced football champion – and to be the winner in a circle of older, bigger, luckier children – that would be thrilling beyond imagination. He hugged his knees together and smiled to himself almost shyly at the thought of so much victory, such laurels.

There he sat smiling, knocking his heels against the bathtub, now and then getting up and going to the door to put his ear to the broad crack and listening for sounds of the game, the pursuer and the pursued, and then returning to his seat with the dogged determination of the true winner, a breaker of records, a champion.

It grew darker in the shed as the light at the door grew softer, fuzzier, turned to a kind of crumbling yellow pollen that turned to yellow fur, blue fur, grey fur. Evening. Twilight. The sound of water gushing, falling. The scent of earth receiving water, slaking its thirst in great gulps and releasing that green scent of freshness, coolness. Through the crack Ravi saw the long purple shadows of the shed and the garage lying still across the yard. Beyond that, the white walls of the house. The bougainvillea had lost its lividity, hung in dark bundles that quaked and twittered and seethed with masses of homing sparrows. The lawn was shut off from his view. Could he hear the children's voices? It seemed to him that he could. It seemed to him that he could hear them chanting, singing, laughing. But what about the game? What had happened? Could it be over? How could it when he was still not found?

It then occurred to him that he could have slipped out long ago, dashed across the yard to the veranda and touched the 'den'. It was necessary to do that to win. He had forgotten. He had only remembered the part of hiding and trying to elude the seeker. He had done that so successfully, his success had occupied him so wholly that he had quite forgotten that success had to be clinched by that final dash to victory and the ringing cry of 'Den!'

With a whimper he burst through the crack, fell on his knees, got up and stumbled on stiff, benumbed legs across the shadowy yard, crying heartily by the time he reached the veranda so that when he flung himself at the white pillar and bawled, 'Den! Den! Den!' his voice broke with rage and pity at the disgrace of it all and he felt himself flooded with tears and misery.

Out on the lawn, the children stopped chanting. They all turned to stare at him in amazement. Their faces were pale and triangular in the dusk. The trees and bushes around them stood inky and sepulchral, spilling long shadows across them. They stared, wondering at his reappearance, his passion, his wild animal howling. His mother rose from her basket chair and came towards him, worried, annoyed, saying, 'Stop it, stop it, Ravi. Don't be a baby. Have you hurt yourself?' Seeing him attended to, the children went back to clasping their hands and chanting 'The grass is green, the rose is red . . .'

But Ravi would not let them. He tore himself out of his mother's grasp and pounded across the lawn into their midst, charging at them with his head lowered so that they scattered in surprise. 'I won, I won, I won,' he bawled, shaking his head so that the big tears flew. 'Raghu didn't find me. I won, I won—'

It took them a minute to grasp what he was saying, even who he was. They had quite forgotten him. Raghu had found all the others long ago. There had been a fight about who was to be It next. It had been so fierce that their mother had emerged from her bath and made them change to another game. Then they had played another and another. Broken mulberries from the tree and eaten them. Helped the driver wash the car when their father returned from work. Helped the gardener water the beds till he roared at them and swore he would complain to their parents. The parents had come out, taken up their positions on the cane chairs. They had begun to play again, sing and chant. All this time no one had remembered Ravi. Having disappeared from the scene, he had disappeared from their minds. Clean.

'Don't be a fool,' Raghu said roughly, pushing him aside, and even Mira said, 'Stop howling, Ravi. If you want to play, you can stand at the end of the line,' and she put him there very firmly.

The game proceeded. Two pairs of arms reached up and met in an arc. The children trooped under it again and again in a lugubrious circle, ducking their heads and intoning

'The grass is green,
The rose is red;
Remember me
When I am dead, dead, dead, dead . . .'

And the arc of thin arms trembled in the twilight, and the heads were bowed so sadly, and their feet tramped to that melancholy refrain so mournfully, so helplessly, that Ravi could not bear it. He would not follow them, he would not be included in this funereal game. He had wanted victory and triumph – not a funeral. But he had been forgotten, left out and he would not join them now. The ignominy of being forgotten – how could he face it? He felt his heart go heavy and ache inside him unbearably. He lay down full length on the damp grass, crushing his face into it, no longer crying, silenced by a terrible sense of his insignificance.

bougainvillea – plant with red or purple flowers
jamun – a kind of nut

A child's eye view

The garden outside was like a tray made of beaten brass, flattened out on the red gravel and stony soil in all shades of metal – aluminium, tin, copper and brass. No life stirred at this arid time of day – the birds drooped, like dead fruit, in the papery tents of the trees . . .

Talk

The first few paragraphs of this story are full of powerful descriptions of a hot Indian garden, like the one in the quotation above. The garden is compared to hot metal because of its colour and because of the heat and light it reflects back at the children. In pairs, make a list of at least three other pieces of description from the opening of the story. For each one talk about what is effective about the words Anita Desai has chosen.

Read

Read these two famous openings of novels. Both show the world from a child's point of view and both make particular use of description.

From *Cider with Rosie*

I was set down from the carrier's cart at the age of three; and there with a sense of bewilderment and terror my life in the village began.

The June grass, amongst which I stood, was taller than I was, and I wept. I had never been so close to grass before. It towered above me and all around me, each blade tattooed with tiger-skins of sunlight. It was knife-edged, dark and a wicked green, thick as a forest and alive with grasshoppers that chirped and chattered and leapt through the air like monkeys.

I was lost and didn't know where to move. A tropic heat oozed up from the ground, rank with sharp odours of roots and nettles. Snow-clouds of elder-blossom banked in the sky, showering upon me the fumes and flakes of their sweet and giddy suffocation. High overhead ran frenzied larks, screaming, as though the sky were tearing apart.

For the first time in my life I was out of the sight of humans. For the first time in my life I was alone in a world whose behaviour I could neither predict nor fathom: a world of birds that squealed, of plants that stank, of insects that sprang about without warning. I was lost and I did not expect to be found again. I put back my head and howled, and the sun hit me smartly on the face, like a bully.

LAURIE LEE

From *Portrait of the Artist as a Young Man*

Once upon a time and a very good time it was there was a moocow coming down along the road and this moocow that was down along the road met a nicens little boy named baby tuckoo . . .

His father told him that story: his father looked at him through a glass: he had a hairy face.

He was baby tuckoo. The moocow came down the road where Betty Byrne lived; she sold lemon platt.

> O, the wild rose blossoms
> On the little green place.

He sang that song. That was his song.

> O, the green wothe botheth.

When you wet the bed first it is warm then it gets cold. His mother put on the oilsheet. That had the queer smell.

His mother had a nicer smell than his father. She played on the piano the sailor's hornpipe for him to dance. He danced:

> Tralala lala,
> Tralala tralaladdy,
> Tralala lala,
> Tralala lala.

JAMES JOYCE

Talk

In pairs:

● briefly describe what you think is happening in *Cider with Rosie* and *Portrait of the Artist as a Young Man*;

● make a list of everything that the two extracts and *Games at Twilight* have in common;

● make a list of all the phrases which you find particularly effective as description. For example: 'tattooed with tiger-skins of light' – you might say that this describes the patterns of brown, black and yellow sunlight which are decorating the grass, that it also makes the grass seem almost human and somehow threatening.

What is particularly striking about the way James Joyce uses language? Choose some examples to make this clear.

Talk about the ways in which in all three pieces the writer makes you aware that you are in a children's world.

Assignment

Write about a powerful childhood memory of your own when you felt excluded, left out or alone. Try to make your description as vivid as possible and to explain the situation which led to your experience.

Children's games

'Let's play hide-and-seek.'
'Who'll be It?'
'You be It.'

'The grass is green,
The rose is red;
Remember me
When I am dead, dead, dead, dead . . .'

Read

Throughout the world children play games from which they gain both pleasure and upset. Read this description of one of the most popular games, Hide-and-Seek.

The simplest form of 'Hide-and-Seek', the stay-where-you-are-until-found variety, is now played mainly by small children, or when only two are playing, or when the game is played indoors. The first person to be found is the seeker in the next game; the last to be found is the winner.

Before the game starts it is necessary to arrange how long the seeker will wait before s/he starts the search. S/he is usually told to count to a hundred. Sometimes the number to be counted is set according to the number of children playing, ten or twenty for each person, and twenty more for the den and twenty more for luck.

In Edinburgh they play 'Vehicles' or 'Buses', the child who is 'it' has to wait where s/he is until a car or van passes by, or – if they are by a main road – until a bus is seen. And in Grimsby they tie the boy or girl to a lamp-post, and he has to escape from this before s/he can start seeking.

Hide-and-Seek becomes more fun, and is considerably speeded up, when the hiders do not remain in their hiding-places, but try to get back to the starting-place unobserved while the seeker is out looking for them.

Even so the game is unsatisfactory. Those who have been found, or who have made their way back safely often get tired of the game before the last person has been found. There is often one clever individual who has hidden in a coal-hole and refuses to come out. After a while the others will grow tired of the game and choose something different to play.

Hide-and-Seek has many different names throughout the world – Cat's Eyes, Run by Dark, Toad in the Hole, Ghosts, Hide and Tick and many more.

In England the game was played back in the sixteenth century, when it was known as 'King'. The first player to reach the base without being caught was known as the king.

The game of Hide-and-Seek was also played in Ancient Greece, so it can realistically be described as being several thousand years old.

ADAPTED FROM *CHILDREN'S GAMES*, IONA AND PETER OPIE

Assignment

Stage 1 Interview a number of older people about the games they remember playing when they were young. Ask them if they have any particularly strong or unusual memories. Ask them to explain how the games were played. Tape-record your interview.

Stage 2 Play back your taped material. Select the parts of it which you find most interesting.

Stage 3 Make a transcript of these extracts.

Stage 4 Write an introduction to your transcripts in which you describe the people you interviewed, what you learned about their childhood and any conclusions you formed.

Stage 5 Produce your final draft.

Teenage games

It is not only children who play these sorts of games. Throughout their lives human beings compete with each other, exclude people from their groups and gang up against each other.

Assignment

Study the following characters. There are five, as there are in Anita Desai's story.

(a) **Gender:** female
    Age: 15
    Family: both parents alive
    one younger brother
    Interests: fashion, pop music, discos
    Special notes: once appeared on TV game show

(b) **Gender:** female
    Age: 15
    Family: only mother alive, no brothers or sisters
    Interests: riding, classical music, ballet
    Special notes: owns her own horse

(c) **Gender:** male
    Age: 16
    Interests: archery, fashion, plays several musical instruments
    Family: both parents alive, youngest of four children (two sisters, one brother)
    Special notes: family recently moved to the area

(d) **Gender:** male
    Age: 15
    Family: parents divorced, lives with father, older sister lives with mother
    Interests: computers
    Special notes: worries about his appearance

(e) **Gender:** female
    Age: 16
    Family: mother works, father looks after the home, one younger sister
    Interests: drama, dance
    Special notes: vegetarian, has wanted to be an actor from early age

Talk

In groups:

● decide on a name for each of the characters;
● talk about the characters and develop them more fully;
● make notes on what you have decided.

Write

Write out a scene in which some or all of these characters meet and exclude one member of the group, like Ravi in *Games at Twilight*.

Stage 1 Decide which of your characters, is going to be excluded from the rest of the group.

Stage 2 Decide where they meet.

Stage 3 Think of an activity they could all join in. Show rivalries between different characters and how one person, in particular, feels left out of the activity.

Additional assignments

NB These might well be suitable for longer studies required by some GCSE examinations or for more independent research.

Assignment 1

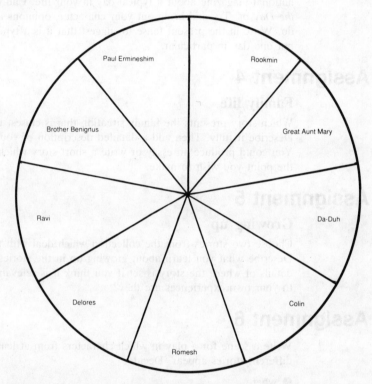

Choose three characters from at least two different stories. Write a diary extract for each character. Imagine, as the character, that you are keeping a private journal of your most personal thoughts. Reflect on the events of one day in the story. In your diary try and bring out what you think your character would have been feeling and why.

Assignment 2

Romesh – Delores – The boy in *Secrets*: difficult decisions

These three characters all have difficult choices to make in their families. Describe the different possible courses of action open to them all and the one actually chosen. What would you have done in the situation? Explain this fully.

Assignment 3

Old age

In *Secrets* and in *To Da-Duh* there are detailed portraits of two old women. What picture of old people do you gain from these two stories? Are there clear differences between Great Aunt Mary and Da-Duh?

Imagine you are either Mary or Da-Duh. Write a feature for a national magazine about a typical day in your life. Call it *A Life in the Day of*. Try and bring out your character, opinions and what you do. Write in the present tense to suggest that it is a typical day and not one day in particular.

Assignment 4

Family life

Which story presents the family situation that is closest to your own? Describe it fully. Then add a detailed description of your own family. You could produce an essay or write a short story which demonstrates the point you wish to make.

Assignment 5

Growing up

Choose two stories from the collection which deal with this subject. Describe what you learn about growing up in the stories. Include details of where the story is set if you think it is relevant. How close to your own experiences are they?

Assignment 6

Write a scene for a play in which characters from at least three different stories appear. Decide:

● where
● why
● on a suitable situation for your scene.

Acknowledgements

The authors would like to thank Elaine and Rosie for their patient understanding.

The authors and publishers wish to thank the following photographic sources:

Sally and Richard Greenhill page 47 top; the Trustees of the Imperial War Museum page 10 top; Popperfoto pages 10 bottom, 47 bottom, 59; John Topham picture Library pages 18, 62, 75, 76, 93, 94.

The publishers have made every effort to trace the copyright holders, but where they have failed to do so they will be pleased to make the necessary arrangements at the first opportunity.

The authors and publishers wish to thank the following who have kindly given permission for the use of copyright material:

The Blackstaff Press for 'Secrets' by Bernard MacLaverty; The English Centre for 'Grandmother' by Sonia Pearce and 'The Beach' by Sarah Wilson from *City Lines*, 1982; Faustin Charles for 'Sugar Cane' from *Breaklight*, ed. Andrew Salkey, Hamish Hamilton, 1971; Victor Gollancz Ltd and the literary executors of Vera Brittain's Estate for extracts from *Chronicle of Youth: Vera Brittain's War Diary 1913–1917*, edited by Alan Bishop; Hamish Hamilton Ltd for material from *Despatches from the Heart* ed. Annette Tapert, 1984; David Higham Associates Ltd on behalf of the author for 'My Grandmother' from *Collected Poems* by Elizabeth Jennings, Macmillan; James MacGibbon for 'Not Waving but Drowning' from *The Collected Poems of Stevie Smith*, Penguin Modern Classics; Deborah Rogers Ltd on behalf of the author for 'Games at Twilight' by Anita Desai from the book of the same name, William Heinemann; Royal Ontario Museum for an extract from *The Indians of Canada: A Survey* by Edward S. Rogers. Copyright © 1970 by The Royal Ontario Museum; *St Thomas Times Journal* for an extract from their December 2nd 1965 issue; George T. Sassoon for 'The Death Bed' by Siegfried Sassoon; Richard Scott Simon Ltd on behalf of the author for 'The Badness Within Him' from *A Bit of Singing and Dancing* by Susan Hill, Hamish Hamilton and Penguin Books; Samuel Selvon for 'Cane is Bitter' from *Best West Indian Stories*, Davis Poynter Ltd; Abner Stein Ltd on behalf of the author for 'The Bottle Queen' from *The Moccasin Telegraph* by W. P. Kinsella, Arena Books; Stoddart Publishing for 'Billie' from *Indians Without Tipis*, edited by Sealey and Kirkness, Irwin Publishing, 1974; Virago Press for an extract from 'To Da Duh, In Memoriam' in *Merle* by Paule Marshall.

Every effort has been made to trace all the copyright holders but if any have been inadvertently overlooked the publishers will be pleased to make the necessary arrangement at the first opportunity.